"I understand." His voice dropped an octave. "Really, I do."

Something about his tone struck Allison. Shane wasn't just sympathetic. There was another layer to his reaction.

Something personal.

Allison chose her words carefully. "I'm glad. Because when it comes to these girls," she fought a rising lump in her throat, "it's important. They deserve way better than what life has given them."

"I can understand that." Shane didn't flinch. "Trust me."

"I do." The quiet words escaped as Allison held Shane's gaze. The moment seized both of them without warning, as strong as a spiritual moment.

Something had happened.

An admission, and a feeling.

And as Allison sat across from this man, she kept her eyes locked on his, not wanting to break it off, even for the briefest of moments.

Audrey Wick is an author and full-time English professor at Blinn College in Texas. Her work has appeared in *Woman's World*, *Chicken Soup for the Soul* and *Writer's Digest*. Audrey believes the secret to happiness includes lifelong learning and good stories—but travel and coffee help. She has journeyed to more than twenty countries and sipped coffee in every one. Connect with her on X and Instagram @WickWrites.

Books by Audrey Wick

Love Inspired

A Home for the Ranger

Visit the Author Profile page at LoveInspired.com.

A HOME FOR THE RANGER

AUDREY WICK

If you purchased this book without a cover you should be aware that this book is stolen property. It was reported as "unsold and destroyed" to the publisher, and neither the author nor the publisher has received any payment for this "stripped book."

ISBN-13: 978-1-335-62130-6

A Home for the Ranger

Copyright © 2025 by Audrey Wick

All rights reserved. No part of this book may be used or reproduced in any manner whatsoever without written permission.

Without limiting the author's and publisher's exclusive rights, any unauthorized use of this publication to train generative artificial intelligence (AI) technologies is expressly prohibited.

This is a work of fiction. Names, characters, places and incidents are either the product of the author's imagination or are used fictitiously. Any resemblance to actual persons, living or dead, businesses, companies, events or locales is entirely coincidental.

For questions and comments about the quality of this book, please contact us at CustomerService@Harlequin.com.

® is a trademark of Harlequin Enterprises ULC.

Love Inspired	HarperCollins Publishers
22 Adelaide St. West, 41st Floor	Macken House, 39/40 Mayor Street Upper,
Toronto, Ontario M5H 4E3, Canada	Dublin 1, D01 C9W8, Ireland
www.LoveInspired.com	www.HarperCollins.com

Printed in Lithuania

While the earth remaineth, seedtime and harvest,
and cold and heat, and summer and winter,
and day and night shall not cease.
—*Genesis* 8:22

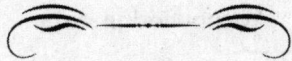

To my Murphy's Writing Retreat friends:
Beth, Janet and Jamie. Thank you for the space to
write, along with the encouragement to attend the
writing conference that led to this publication.

Acknowledgments:

During a writing conference in New Orleans,
I connected with Melissa Endlich, whose enthusiasm
for this story and support of my writing made this
book possible. It's been a joy to work with you and the
Harlequin team to bring fictional Cottonwood Creek
to readers. Thank you for saying "yes!" to my writing.

Beth Wiseman, our shared experiences in
New Orleans along with you being an early
champion of this manuscript helped me immensely.
Continued gratitude for your mentorship and support!

Finally, many years of hiking, walking and outdoor
exploring informed my descriptions of place in this
story, and I've loved having a partner through it all.
Thank you, Brian, for countless shared experiences
and the encouragement of writing along the way.

Chapter One

With one hand touching the cell phone in his shirt pocket and the other on the stocked utility belt at his hip, Park Ranger Shane Hutton raced toward the frantic cries coming from the switchback.

"Is anyone hurt?" he yelled while picking up speed on the downhill slope of the trail when he heard another scream.

"Snake!" A blonde woman was headed straight for him, another hopped a fencepost railing and a third disappeared around a lower curve of the trail.

"Is anyone bit?" he called, slowing just enough so he didn't collide with the one who looked ready to jump into his arms. Her legs moved fast enough to ensure she landed behind something protective.

Which, for the time being, was Shane.

She crouched low and peeked around his body. "It's at the edge." She eased just enough to point a finger down the trail, her hand shaking like a leaf. "Right there!"

Shane's priority was safety, but there was no one writhing in pain or clutching an ankle, which meant no one was bit.

Just frightened.

He slid his hand from his belt, straightening his posture in a man-to-beast showdown. The snake lay like a discarded piece of ribbon across the dirt trail. The slight tilt of its head was the only indication that it was alive.

"Please tell me you are going to do something with that." The blonde woman's voice lowered an octave but still cracked.

"I take it you don't care for snakes?" Shane took a step toward the culprit, its diamond-shaped pattern a dead giveaway as to its species.

A copperhead.

Native—and poisonous.

But also docile.

"They're more scared of you than you are of them." He had uttered that phrase countless times over the course of his five-year career.

"I doubt that," one of the women called from the brush, her voice trembling with an aftershock of fear.

But what was there to do? He was a ranger, not a wildlife expert.

"You better do something," the one farthest from him insisted. Then her head snapped hard to the right. "Slow down," she warned someone Shane couldn't see. "Snake!"

A fourth woman bounded into view, her brunette ponytail swinging in time with her footfalls. She jogged to a stop and popped an earbud out of her ear. "Sorry." She apologized to no one and everyone as she gave her running shoes a rest. "Everything okay?"

"Don't step on—" The woman closest to her brought her fist to her mouth and let out another low squeal.

"Oh," the ponytailed runner said. She removed her second earbud as she came within two feet of the snake. "Hey there, buddy." She dipped slightly at the waist, taking in the sight that sent the other women bursting away like fireworks.

"Taking a little sun bath today?" She righted her posture and rested a hand on her hip.

The cute exchange and playful tone was the complete opposite of the other women. This was a trail runner who reacted to nature in the way that Shane did: naturally.

Mother Nature had her own ebb and flow. Listening to her rhythm and respecting her boundaries was an important part of his job.

The runner shielded her eyes and looked to Shane, picking up the conversation as if it were just the two of them. "It's unusual for a copperhead to be out during the day. This time of year, they should only be nocturnal."

Impressed by her knowledge, he noted, "That's right."

She brought her hand down. "But this one looks to be a youngster." She shrugged. "Go on, little buddy," she urged with a singsong voice that indicated she could keep calm under pressure. She respected the snake's right to cross the path by not making any threatening movements. As if soothed by her presence and heeding her permission, the snake slithered on its way, soundless as a breeze.

The ponytailed snake charmer looked up, a hint of late-afternoon sunshine lighting her face in a luminous glow.

"It's a great day for a run," Shane offered.

"Every day's a great day for a run." She squinted her bright blue eyes at him. "Even when there's a minor interruption on the trail." The corners of her eyes creased with laugh lines that reminded Shane of the lightheartedness of the scene.

No one was hurt.

No one was in danger.

And his own spike of adrenaline was dissipating. "You're right about that."

"I'm Allison." She nodded her hello. "You must be the new ranger I've been hearing about?"

"Good things, I hope." He returned the nod. "I'm Shane Hutton."

"Welcome to the area. I run here regularly. It's my favorite place to do so for the hill country views alone."

"Cottonwood Creek State Park brings lots of visitors to the area for a reason." He looked back to the group of women, who seemed to have calmed down.

"I'll be on my way, then." As rapidly as Allison had been interrupted, she resumed her routine. "Have a great rest of your hike, everyone." She waved before popping her earbuds back into place. To Shane, she flashed a wide smile, effervescent as a model in a toothpaste commercial. He moved back just enough to let her pass with high-step strides as she made her way up the incline of the switchback trail that zagged to and fro toward an ascent.

Shane's gaze lingered a beat longer than was necessary as she rounded one of the hairpin turns, tracing back in the direction he had first arrived from. She moved with a litheness that was mesmerizing.

But then the trio of scared women snapped him back to duty. "That nearly gave me a heart attack." The blonde placed her hand over her heart.

"You're too young for that, honey," her friend insisted. Slowly, the women reformed their small group, resuming their hike along the trail.

Shane was confident they could take care of themselves and told them so. Still, he offered to accompany them to the trailhead. "It's just around a couple more bends."

"I won't say no to that." The blonde pivoted and told Shane, "Lead the way." He shepherded the women, taking the first step. Soon, they were back on track, the women's reptile encounter in their rearview mirror.

They wound their way beside views that showcased the small town of Cottonwood Creek below the park, which sat in the valley beneath high limestone bluffs. Through trees and foliage, Shane could see the bakery, the barbecue joint, the community hospital, churches and the school. While the views were beautiful, they were not as desolate as he would like.

When the interim head ranger position became open, Shane had put in for it, hoped that he'd get it, but didn't think too much else about it.

His goal, after all, wasn't Cottonwood Creek.

It was much farther west in the state.

Wide-open west Texas was where he wanted to be. It was what called to his soul.

He longed for something that he could only describe as the same longing that cowboys who once roamed the open range felt. He wanted natural spaces where streets and fences didn't cut across every few acres. Mountains that reached into big Texas skies. Unspoiled land where he could feel swallowed. He liked helping people at parks, but he wanted to do so on a much grander, remote scale.

For now, he was at Cottonwood Creek. And with each footfall, a fresh memory pounded into Shane's subconscious and became one he couldn't shake. It was the singular image of the confident, ponytailed runner who appeared like a dream yet disappeared as quickly as one.

Allison Van Horn kept her breathing steady as her running shoes gripped the trail.

One, two.

One, two.

Placing one foot in front of the other was a type of meditation for her. Running gave Allison a measured task on which to focus, which helped clear her brain fog after a busy workday.

And after the week she'd been having at work, she needed it. Medical office billing had no slow season.

Once at the top of the trail, she took a deep breath and sprinted on the straightaway that led her beneath a canopy of namesake cottonwood trees with stately trunks and large, sweeping limbs that arched above. Their fluffy, cotton-like tufts in bloom spread across broad, flat leaves, creating shade and a magical effect. The trees had to be twice as old as she was. Maybe more. At twenty-four, she felt like a sapling next to them.

Allison raised the back of her hand to her forehead, wiping away the sweat there.

Just a few more yards.

She kept her stride even and her balance steady as she ended her trail run. She rocked her wrist to activate the digital display of her smartwatch.

3.1 miles.

That was the equivalent of a 5K run, which was her goal twice a week after work. She tapped the display to check her time.

Decent.

Especially considering that interruption.

Since she hadn't seen any more commotion or heard any screams over her music, she assumed the women were all okay after their encounter with a snake. Copperheads may look menacing, but it was unusual for them to strike. The women had nothing to worry about.

Besides, they were now in the company of a park ranger,

one whose handsome profile and strong jawline Allison couldn't help but remember.

Awareness ran up her spine as she recalled meeting Shane.

She dropped her arm, rolled back her shoulders and lifted her head skyward. Placing both hands on her hips, she walked to regain her breath and slow her heartbeat.

The split seconds after a 5K always flooded her with a mixture of weariness and energy. The muscles in her legs burned from the switchbacks, her heart thudded wildly, yet the sensations were her body's way of telling her she was alive.

Capable.

And able to handle more than she thought possible.

It had been a good run.

She detoured to a water fountain, then ducked into the park's restrooms. She leaned over the sink, twisted the faucet and splashed a bit of cool water on her face and the back of her neck. Then she patted her cheeks and chin with a paper towel.

Refreshed, she rounded the corner of the building to walk past the welcome window of the park's main headquarters—and there he was.

Again.

Through the glass, his Texas Parks and Wildlife Department badge shone, pinned to one side of his chest while his name tag anchored the other.

She missed the kind-eyed Mr. Atacosta, who had held the head ranger position at Cottonwood Creek for the past twenty years. Allison had heard him say it was an easy gig. Mother Nature, after all, took care of herself. But Mr. Atacosta had also spoken to Allison about his worries of the cash-strapped Texas park system and whether the state would invest in a quality replacement for him.

Shane didn't look a thing like his predecessor and must have been a third of his age. He slid open the window so he could talk to Allison. "Hey, there. Thanks for your help back on the trails."

"Oh, I don't know that I was much help."

"Sure you were," he insisted. He lowered his voice almost to a whisper. "Those women were ready to climb the trees after seeing that snake."

"I saw the shoes they were wearing. They wouldn't have made it very far up any kind of tree."

"True." Shane smiled. "It's a pleasure to meet a regular park guest." He stuck out his hand.

Allison rubbed the palm of her hand against her running shorts, a bit embarrassed at the sweat, though she reciprocated. Even through the heat from her workout, her skin flushed beneath his grip. "You're the replacement for Mr. Atacosta?"

"Temporarily."

"Oh?" Allison withdrew her hand.

"I'm just the interim ranger until the park system decides on a permanent replacement."

"I see."

"So how was your run?"

"Hot." It was an honest appraisal.

"Today is unusually warm for May." Shane leaned forward, his broad shoulders framing an athletic build, evident even in spite of his uniform. "Especially with the temperatures we had just a few days ago, and the rain."

There was a mugginess to the air and a humidity that, while good for her skin, did make today's run a bit harder than it should have been. "Texas," Allison replied, shrugging.

"That's right. What's the saying?" Shane answered his

own question. "If you don't like the weather, then wait awhile. It'll change."

"That's exactly right." Allison had been following that tenet her whole life. "I'm Texas born and bred."

"Me, too." Shane leaned in. "You said you live here in Cottonwood Creek?"

"Yes." She stowed her earbuds in the pocket of her running shorts. "Grew up here. Moved away for two years of college to get a medical certification, but I came back to be close to my family and friends. I work at the Lone Star Medical Clinic."

"Are you a nurse?"

Allison cringed, hating when people made that assumption. "No. I work in Billing."

"Oh."

That was usually the reaction she got. But Shane surprised her.

"Then you get the honor of following up with patients, making sure they're okay. That's got to make you smile."

"Actually, it does." Those weren't the exact words that came to mind regarding her duties, but they were an extension of it. Her work was important, and she took pride in it. Medical coding and billing, after all, was a unique skill set. It was nice that someone recognized that.

Shane held her eye contact, a penetrating gaze of interest that moved beyond casual. This new ranger was looking at her the way one of the rural resident doctors-in-training had done six months ago.

Before the would-be doctor asked her on a date.

That relationship had broken her heart. If Shane thought he could capture her interest with a stare, he was in for a surprise.

16   *A Home for the Ranger*

Because Allison Van Horn had something else in mind. "How long is your interim appointment at the park?"

"Four months."

Perfect timing. Allison's idea lifted like a blanket being raised in the wind. Slowly, the four corners of it came together. If she didn't seize this opportunity, she'd regret it later.

"I'd like to make a request. Could I reserve the pavilion for the first Saturday in June?"

Shane nodded. "No problem. The office manager, Nadine, has already left for the day, but she'll be back in the morning. She's the one who can help you with that."

Allison knew all about the responsibilities of longtime employee, Nadine Kreische. Not only had Allison flashed her park pass to her countless times, but she also knew her as a patient from the clinic. And while Allison could have asked Nadine questions about the pavilion's availability, she needed the one who controlled the purse strings of the park to approve her request. In the past, that would have been Mr. Atacosta. Now it was Shane. "I want to ask you for a special favor regarding the reservation."

"Oh?" Shane arched an eyebrow, giving her a sidelong glance that made her breath catch.

There was no easy way to do this. Like ripping off a bandage, the best technique would be the swiftest one. "To be frank, I don't have money to spend on the rental. And the party's not for me. It's for two little girls who are turning six years old."

Shane's expression softened. "A kid's party, then. How many guests are we talking about?"

His question offered promise. She was reeling him in, at least enough to continue the conversation. "Not many."

Allison did a quick mental calculation. "Maybe two dozen people or so. And most of those will be adults," she clarified.

"At a kids' birthday party?"

"Yes." Allison fought the urge to tell the story of twin girls, Olivia and Isla, who felt like family to her. The twins had been placed with a Cottonwood Creek foster couple a few months ago, after being removed from an unsafe home environment in another town, and they were awaiting next steps. While they had a foster mother and father at the moment, the CASA program for Court Appointed Special Advocates helped with stability outside of that. Allison was their advocate during legal proceedings, meaning she was present by proxy in the courtroom so they didn't have to be there in person. Additionally, she served as a mentor to them, kind of like a fun aunt to keep their minds off the hard parts of their lives.

Multiple times a week after work and every Saturday, she spent time with them. In cooperation with their foster parents, she aimed to give the twins quality attention from someone who could be a steady, guiding presence in their lives. She had thrown herself into the volunteer job as a way to heal her own broken heart.

Fiercely protective of their privacy but wanting to fight for their best interests, she asked again. "Could it be possible for me to use the pavilion free of charge? I promise that, if you agree to this, we'll be in and out in two hours, tops. We'll clean up after ourselves. No confetti. No glitter. No mess."

How else could she sweeten the deal?

Advocacy had become part of Allison's life, the twins' needs intertwining with her day-to-day schedule in ways she could never have predicted before they landed in her life. She wanted to give them a sense of normalcy. Plus, to help ease the responsibility of care after their placement in a home that had other children, she told their foster parents that she would handle the party. For their upcoming birthday, that was the best present she could offer.

Shane didn't break her gaze. "Will there be cake?"

Allison cut her eyes at him. "It's a birthday celebration. Of course there will be cake." Cake was a necessity. So were decorations and party hats. Then there were gifts for the girls. They didn't need to be extravagant, but she couldn't throw them a party and forgo presents. With all of these costs, Allison's budget was stretched thin.

But she wouldn't let these girls go without, not if she could help it.

"Good." Shane gave a curt nod. "Because for a minute there, it sounded like your party would be no fun." The corner of his mouth curved into a sly smile.

Allison's heart was on the cusp of swelling with gratitude. "Is that a yes?" All she needed was a yes.

But she couldn't strong-arm Shane into this decision. He shook his head. As quickly as the door of possibility had opened, it slammed shut. "I'm sorry, but I can't let you use the pavilion for free."

"But you have to understand the circumstances." Allison started to protest, but then swallowed the rest of her sentence. She couldn't expose the girls' history, even if this request was in their best interest.

"Look, I'd like to help you out." Shane tilted his head, his earlier promise evaporating with every word he spoke. "But I've got to do things by the book. There's protocol to follow and as much as I'd like to bend the rules, I can't do that on my first week. Not when it involves money collection."

"I respect that." Still, it didn't lessen the sting of an answer she didn't want to hear.

"If you want to have a get-together without a rental cost,

there's no reason you can't grab a couple of picnic tables by the lake." He gestured vaguely in their direction. "But it's first come, first serve."

"Right." And there was no shade, no restrooms nearby and no electricity. Tying a few balloons to a picnic bench wouldn't be the same as a fully decorated venue. "I understand." The party needed to be memorable and meaningful.

Because this wasn't just an annual gathering.

This was a party for two girls who never before had anyone celebrate their birthday.

Allison wouldn't give up on them. She'd do everything in her power to protect and support them. No matter what.

Chapter Two

Allison closed the door of her Honda, hearing a chatter of voices carrying over from the backyard of Mia and Michael Westmoreland's home. She had been there so often the past few months as she spent time with the twins that she was comfortable coming and going like family, though Mia had always made her feel like that. Their friendship had been years in the making, ever since they met at the medical clinic where the entire Westmoreland family were patients.

Allison stepped to the metal fencing, waving first to Mia and then Michael, who was kicking a soccer ball back and forth with kids in a wide circle. Allison recognized the older three, who ranged in age from ten to six. Olivia and Isla, with their wavy brown hair and petite frames, may have looked different from the Westmoreland kids, but they were included in the fun just the same.

The twins looked up as Allison called to them. "Olivia. Isla. Are you ready to go?" Her voice sang out across the neat but toy-cluttered backyard.

The five-year-olds raced over to Allison, picking up a puppy on the way, who was no bigger than a shoebox. Olivia was the first to ask, "Can we take him with us?"

"Pretty please?" Isla echoed Olivia, raising the adorable ball of fur. One ear stood at attention as the other folded and flopped. His huge, saucer-shaped eyes took the phrase *puppy dog eyes* to a whole new level.

"He really wants to come with us."

"I bet he does." It broke Allison's heart to have to tell the girls, "I'm sorry, but Lucky can't come with us."

Isla pouted and hugged Lucky to her chest. "Sorry, buddy."

"Maybe another time," Allison added, though she knew better than to make promises to the girls. They barely saw past each school day, had little concept of calendar time and they were still learning how to interact with adults.

For that matter, she was still learning how to interact with them. Without the support of fellow volunteers—the very ones who got her through Court Appointed Special Advocates training and certification—she would never have had the courage to take on one child, never mind two at once.

But the moment her eyes fell on Olivia and Isla, she melted. The girls' father had abandoned them when they were too young to remember, which was a part of their story that especially resonated with Allison.

Her own father had left, too.

The difference? Allison was old enough to remember.

The twins had been raised by their mother, but in an unsafe environment. Months of wellness calls finally culminated in their mother being arrested. The official charge was drug-related, and since it involved manufacturing, she would be behind bars for a long time.

The girls had been placed in the foster system while a suitable next-of-kin could be located. Except no one had materialized. Not anyone, at least, who was willing to take on the responsibilities of twins.

That was when foster parents Mia and Michael had stepped in to help. With roots deep in the community, they anchored the girls. In Cottonwood Creek, people took care of one another.

Developmentally, Olivia and Isla were behind expectations for their age. Their mother had neglected their medical care and never enrolled them in any preschool or public school program.

But under the care of Mia and Michael, in cooperation with oversight from CASA, the girls had made incredible strides. They received care at Lone Star Clinic and had been in school for the first time this year. Allison noticed advancement every time she saw them. Being around Mia and Michael's other three children no doubt helped.

Mia came to the fence. "Thanks so much for taking them to the park today. They've been talking about it for hours."

"I've been looking forward to this Saturday with them. And to giving you a break."

"Thank you for that." Mia brought a hand to her temple, massaging as she said, "Let me walk with them to your car. Girls?" she called to them as they were getting Lucky situated. "Are you ready?"

Isla lowered the puppy into the grass, hind legs first. "There you go," she coached as he got his bearings. "We'll be back later. Be a good boy."

Olivia blew Lucky a kiss as he raced to Michael and the kids, eager for more attention. Olivia then bounded to Mia's side. "I'm ready." She beamed across the fence.

"Me, too!" Isla joined her.

At times, Allison was a tad overwhelmed by the girls. Two bundles of energy, she needed two sets of eyes to watch them because they had double the needs. They also had double the amount to say and double the number of questions to ask. And, because of their past, the twins needed double the attention.

But when they looked at her with such sweet, expectant faces, they were also doubly cute.

Allison opened the gate for the girls, ushering them through while Lucky stayed safely behind in the backyard. The puppy whimpered just once before Michael scooped him up and waved goodbye to everyone, adding an exaggerated paw wave from Lucky that made the girls giggle.

As Mia ushered the twins through the gate, Allison extended her hands, Isla clasping first before Olivia did the same. She squeezed a quick pulse of reassurance to them both. "We're going to have a great afternoon."

"The best!" the girls sang in happy refrain.

Yes, two young girls demanded a lot of attention. And Allison may not have two of everything. But she had one caring heart. And sometimes, that alone made all the difference.

Both women helped the girls into Allison's car, buckling them into booster seats. "Comfy?"

"Just like your car, Miss Mia." That was what the girls had taken to calling their foster mom, which Allison thought was appropriate.

Their biological mom was going to be in prison for so long that the girls probably wouldn't see her out of jail until they were old enough to be mothers themselves.

If they ever saw her, because according to the girls' case files, the mother was interested in terminating her rights. But neither Allison nor Mia was about to share that with the girls. They were too young to understand. Plus, Allison's role wasn't in deciding their future. Hers, instead, was a support role. She kept an eye on their well-being, looked out for their best interests and loved them.

Her heart sang around them, and their time together was more than forced volunteerism. It was a tender expression of care steeped in respect for their welfare.

She settled herself into the driver's seat, giving the duo a glance in the rearview mirror. "Ready?"

"Ready, Freddy!" They giggled.

Allison shook her head. She never quite knew what would come out of their little mouths.

That was part of the fun of spending time with them. With Allison, the girls could be themselves. She started the ignition, shifted the car into Reverse and waved as Mia saw them off.

Before they were out of the driveway, Olivia asked, "So where are we going again?"

"It's a park. I go there all the time."

"Do they have a playground?"

Of course that would be their priority. "Not exactly. But they do have a couple of swing sets."

"That's not the same thing." Olivia crossed her arms over her chest.

"You're right." Allison kept her eyes on the road but stole glances through the mirror. The girls had been placed in Cottonwood Creek due to the availability of the Westmorelands' foster home, but the town itself was still very new to them. "But people go to this park for reasons besides the swing sets."

"What else do they do there?"

Allison didn't want to spoil all the surprises she had planned, but she told them a little bit. "Well, they go on nature walks. Explore trails. Look at wildflowers." As she said the things she enjoyed most about the park, she realized how boring these probably sounded to five-year-olds, so she added, "There's also a lake where we can rent pedal boats."

"What's a pedal boat?"

Naturally, she chastised herself. Why would a five-year-old know that? "It's a small boat that doesn't have a sail or a motor. You have to sit and move your feet along pedals that help the boat to go."

"Like a bike?"

"Exactly like a bike."

"And then what do we do?"

Allison would answer questions for the entire ride if she wasn't careful. "You'll see when we get there."

That seemed to appease them enough for the time being. Then she changed the subject. "How about some music?"

"Yes!" They pumped their fists into the air and kicked their legs as she found a Christian radio station. What a blessing because she had no way of knowing when she bought the used Honda before she started college that she would one day be headed out on a Saturday with two twin girls in the backseat.

Their heads bopped happily along with a song they didn't seem to know but appreciated. The music helped Allison relax, too. After all, today was all about having fun. She needed to remember that as much for the girls' sakes as her own.

And if things went well, she might be able to convince the park ranger regarding the birthday party. After all, how could he say no once he saw the faces of these two?

Unless he was as slithering as that snake on the path when she first encountered him. Allison loved all of God's creatures, as long as they had a heart.

Surely, this man had a heart, too. Maybe it just needed a wake-up call.

"We're here, girls." She pulled into the parking lot and chose a spot beneath the shade of a tree. The girls released the seat belts of their booster seats in a flash.

"Let's go," Olivia called to Isla, urging her out the door that Allison held open.

"We're so excited," Isla spoke for her sister. They adored the outdoors.

Seeing their happiness made her think again of the party possibilities. Maybe she could spring for the cost of the pavilion after all. It might mean eating a few more peanut butter sandwiches at lunch for a couple of weeks, but that was a small price to pay.

But she didn't need to think about that now. She tried to push disappointment from her mind as she and the girls wound their way along a curved sidewalk to the park's front entrance window. Allison fished her annual park pass from her wallet, explaining to the girls how the entry fees worked. "But this card means that we don't have to pay anything today. This card gets us in."

They oohed when she plucked the card and slanted it to catch the glint of the sunlight. The girls wanted to hold the card.

"First, we have to show it to the people that work here." She stepped to the front of the headquarters window, expecting she might see one of the rangers due to the time of day. At the thought that it might be Shane, a fluttery mixture of nervous apprehension filled her chest.

But it didn't flutter for long.

Nadine slid open the entrance window. "Hello, Allison."

"Hi, Nadine." She flashed her pass. Doing so was a matter of protocol, and Nadine was a rule follower. She nodded, which was Allison's cue to stow the pass. "Thanks," she said, but not before handing it to the girls to turn over and inspect. They passed it between them as Allison continued to talk with Nadine.

"My pleasure." Nadine logged their attendance with a couple of keystrokes on the nearby computer. Allison admired that Nadine was so orderly and methodical.

Maybe that was why the new ranger was walking a straight line. He might be the boss, but Nadine really ran the show.

"I brought along a couple of guests today." Allison nodded toward the girls.

"I see that." Nadine waved to the pint-size parkgoers. "Welcome to Cottonwood Creek State Park, ladies. Have you ever been here before?"

"No, ma'am." The girls handed the pass back to Allison and looked around wide-eyed, their gazes darting from colorful signage to the enticing neon trail maps to a set of wooden stairs that led down an embankment and to the lake, just visible in the distance.

"Well, you're going to love it," she assured them. "Plus, you've got one of our best guests showing you around."

"Is there a playground here?"

Allison winced at the question before softening. She had to remind herself that children's memories were sometimes like sieves.

"No, sweetie," Nadine jumped in. "We don't have that here. Just some swings. But this whole park can be your playground." She extended her arms in a broad gesture of welcome.

"Thank you, Nadine. Come on, girls." She positioned herself between the girls and extended her hands. "We can check out the swings first. Then the pedal boats."

She wanted to take advantage of the water recreation, but there was no way she'd host the girls' birthday at the lake. She still had her eye on the pavilion. And one way or another, she was going to make that happen.

Shane heard Nadine through the thin walls of his office. He touched his fingers to his forehead, massaging away the tension that had built up from his morning.

She poked her head around the corner. "You need to eat something," Nadine counseled with the care of a mother.

She was one. Just not Shane's.

"Thanks," he said. "But I'm fine."

"Did you have lunch?"

"No."

"Why not?"

Because I was dealing with a tour group.

Because I got a radio call at the lake.

Because the grounds staff needed help clearing trail debris.

Instead of listing all his tasks—which were never the same day to day—he settled on, "Regular meals aren't my priority."

"Well, maybe they should be." Nadine eyed him like a fish she had just pulled from a line. "Because you're looking a little thin."

"You've only known me for a week."

She shrugged. "As much good food as we have around central Texas, you should be fattening up. Even after a week."

"We have good food where I'm from in east Texas, too."

Nadine guffawed, choking on words she didn't say.

He read the subtext. "We do."

"Don't tell tall tales." She wagged a finger at him.

"It's not a tale. It's true."

"Fine." She leaned back on her heel, yielding the floor to him. "Go ahead."

He cocked his head and looked at her. "You want me to talk about food when I haven't even had any lunch?"

"So you *are* hungry." She raised her finger as if she were a detective who had just discovered a clue.

"Yes," he granted with a heavy sigh. "I'm hungry."

"Then why didn't you just say so? Go take your lunch

out by the lake. Too pretty of a day to eat in the break room anyway." She held a twinkle in her eye, one Shane couldn't read fully.

"Is there some reason you want me to head out there?"

She lowered her glasses with one hand and touched her chest with the other. "Who, me?"

"You're hiding something."

Shane was supposed to be the one in charge, but Nadine had worked at the park for almost as many years as he'd been alive. She was like a second mother to the staff, who respected her. Shane did, too, for her no-nonsense work ethic.

But he was still learning how to handle her sass.

"Fine. I'll be back in thirty minutes."

"You're allowed an hour."

"I don't need it."

Shane walked to the break room, grabbed his brown bag lunch from the refrigerator and escaped out the back door of the headquarters. After making his way around the side of the building, he descended the wooden steps that led to the unshaded trail and to the park's only lake, a small but serene spot.

Cottonwood Creek Lake.

A picture from the trailhead that showed the lake at sunset was what captured him the most when he researched the park online prior to applying for the position. Today it was as gorgeous as the photograph, minus the setting sun. It certainly was prettier than some of the dank, swampy ones around his childhood home in east Texas.

The Piney Woods area where he was raised held secrets of both geography and people, including some from his parents that led to a feeling of distance with them both. He had tried to talk to God about the wedge in their relationship for years, though answers weren't materializing.

Shane was their only biological child, but he never felt like enough for them. He tightened his grip on the top of his lunch bag, needing an outlet for hurtful memories he would deal with another time.

Shane tamped them down as he let landscape views of the park's lake refocus his attention.

Few state parks in Texas had a lake, and even though this one was small, it was well used. Comfortable picnic tables dotted one corner of the lake. A small shed stood on the opposite side, a landing spot for pedal boats that were rented from the park headquarters. There were usually no more than a half dozen on the water, if that many. Today there were only two, cutting through the placid surface.

Shane settled at a picnic table, unwrapped his barbecue sandwich and opened his bag of kettle chips. He ate in silence, save for the sweep of the breeze and the occasional laughter carrying over from the park patrons enjoying the boats.

He palmed an orange he had tossed into the bag at the last minute, digging his thumbnail into the flesh and releasing the tangy aroma into the already sweet spring air. As he ate, his attention was caught by a trio of voices that were coming down the trail, life jackets already in hand.

Nadine wore many hats at the headquarters, and fitting pedal-boat-goers for life jackets was just one of them. Shane smiled to himself because she must have had fun in this particular instance. Two little girls, mirror images of each other, carried their jackets with the pride of trophies. Their pace quickened as they neared the bank of the lake, and the woman grabbed one by the shoulder while the other lurched just out of reach. "Don't. Not yet."

Luckily, the second girl stopped. The woman knelt, seemed to be telling them something and then helped each girl into her life jacket. When she stood, she shielded her eyes with her hand as she gazed over the lake.

The stance. The ponytail. The lithe figure of a runner.

It was Allison.

He raised a hand in greeting, and she returned the gesture.

So did the little girls, waving as if they were at a parade. They wobbled in the life jackets that made them look like miniature sumo wrestlers, bumping shoulders and pushing out their bellies as they seemed to consider these new additions.

Allison's head then snapped from the pedal boats to the shed to the water and back again.

She could probably use some help. Shane popped the last orange segment into his mouth, tossed the rind into the bag and eased up from his bench. He gave her another wave to signify he was coming over.

When he made his way to the trio, one of the girls called out first. "We're going swimming."

"No, we're not," Allison said. "No swimming."

"Oh." The girl's face fell.

Her sister came to her rescue. "Don't you remember? We're going in a boat," she announced happily.

"That's right." The first girl's face lifted.

Their words were rapid-fire, as if they only operated at a single speed. Fast.

And from the worried look on Allison's face, they probably did. She skipped the formality of introductions. "Tell me if this is a bad idea."

Shane chuckled. "Depends if their legs can reach the pedals." Though even if they couldn't, it didn't take much force to propel the tiny boats. One person could do it.

The girls bounced around in circles. "We can do it," they insisted.

"I just don't know if I can," Allison muttered under her breath, though clear enough for Shane to hear.

"You okay?" If she had a fear of water, this probably wasn't the best decision.

"I'm just worried about the steadiness of the boat out there."

Shane understood. "I can help with that." The boat had four seats that sat back-to-back. Pedals were only in front, so he explained, "You'll want to be in front to power the boat. Then the girls can be in back to balance." He held two fingers on each hand in front of him, mimicking the four seats of the boat. He wobbled them back and forth. "That way, the pedal boat will stay stable."

"I assumed we could just all sit together," Allison whispered quietly.

He assured her, "Once you get settled, you'll be fine. I'll help."

"Are you going with us?" The girls looked to him expectantly.

"Because you need a life jacket," one of them insisted.

Shane had only intended to help them get seated and then he'd launch the boat. But at the girls' words, he looked to Allison for how to respond. She simply cocked her head as if to say, "Safety first."

True, he probably needed to be a good role model for these girls, even if he was only helping them from the bank. "I can get one from the shed." Extras were kept there for staff.

He had the girls pick out a boat as he threw away his lunch bag, retrieved a jacket and returned to find them poised around their choice.

"It looks like a Popsicle!" one of the girls proclaimed with pride of the orange-and-white four-seater.

"Well…" Shane struggled with how to talk to children, especially two at the same time. "Do you like Popsicles?"

"Yes!"

Awkwardly, he tried to keep the conversation going, but found it more difficult than he'd imagined.

Why was talking to kids so tough?

Rattled, he turned his attention toward the boat. "I want you to sit here—" he pointed to one of the backward-facing seats as he directed the girls "—and you to sit here."

But Allison cut in. "I don't like the thought of one of them being just outside my reach."

"Weight needs to be evenly distributed," he reminded her. Pairing the girls in back with Allison as the adult in front was the only way.

Allison chewed her bottom lip. "What if they share the passenger's seat?"

Each bucket seat was made for one. "I wouldn't recommend it."

"Or you can come along." The simple solution was delivered from the mouth of the young problem solver swifter than an axe chop.

Two adults. Two children. Four seats. It did make sense.

Allison's worried look washed away as she asked sheepishly, "Will you?"

Shane didn't want to leave Allison in a lurch. He glanced at his watch. He hadn't even taken thirty minutes yet for lunch. And he did have a life jacket. Besides, this was work related, wasn't it? "Just enough to get you settled out there. Then you can drop me off and have the rest of the afternoon to yourself."

Allison brought her hands to a steeple position and rested them just below her chin. "Thank you," she mouthed.

He raised his hands. "Launch time."

Chapter Three

Allison hadn't thought this excursion through enough. She had seen these pedal boats so often that she assumed they would make an amusing addition to the girls' park visit. But she hadn't considered all the logistics.

Wiggly movements from five-year-olds couldn't always be predicted. Had it been just the three of them in the boat, one of the girls would have been too far from Allison's grasp. In terms of safety, that made Allison's heart palpitate.

Luckily, there was someone there to help. Thanks to Shane, they were able to each take a front seat yet stay within arm's reach of the girls in the rear-facing ones. The boat was balanced with an adult and child each on one side, sitting back-to-back.

Safe. And stable.

A wave of relief crested over Allison just knowing there would be another adult by her side. Because if anything were to happen to the girls on her watch, she couldn't live with herself.

"Are we ready to go?" Shane stood with boots on the grassy bank and hands on the rub rail of the boat.

"Ready, Freddy!" the girls cheered. They were already having fun, which made Allison loosen up a bit. She looked to Shane, who was cracking a smile at their antics. "Go, go, go." The girls clapped their hands to spur him on with the launch.

After one swift push, the vessel glided away from the bank. Shane eased into the front seat the split second before it fully entered the water, careful not to rock the boat as he settled into his seat. "And we're off," he announced.

The girls graced him with applause. They were nothing if not appreciative.

Shane pretended to tip his hat to them. The girls didn't quite get it, but Allison welcomed his lighthearted humor.

She adjusted her feet to the pedals and applied gentle pressure as Shane did the same on his side. Pedaling wasn't nearly as tough as she suspected it might be. Churning smooth as butter, they propelled the boat forward.

"What do you think, girls?" she called over her shoulder.

Their giggles of glee said it all.

"I'll take that as a win." Shane settled farther into his seat. "Now, I should probably be introduced to these two."

"Oh my, where are my manners?" Allison gasped.

"Don't worry about it." He waved innocuously, as if this was any other routine meeting.

Allison pointed with her thumb to the girls in back. "Olivia," she prompted, and the girl closest to her waved as Shane turned around to see them. "And Isla. Meet Park Ranger Hutton."

"Calling me Shane is fine."

An echo of "hi" floated his way, along with a full statement of gratitude from one of the girls. "Thanks for the boat, Mr. Shane."

"Well, it's not mine..." Shane started to say, but then he stopped and said, "You're welcome." He leaned into Allison and asked, "How do you tell them apart?"

"Mannerisms, mostly." It had taken Allison a while to know one from the other. Of course, their personalities were very different. Isla was more outspoken, Olivia slightly more reserved and shy. Olivia was also more emotional whereas Isla had a grit about her that could sometimes border on stubbornness. They were both strong-willed, but they were wholly capable of love.

Allison had seen it firsthand. The girls loved their mother and father, even though they both were out of the picture right now. They spoke of them—often without warning—and Allison simply let the words and memories flow when they did. She wasn't their counselor or their pastor, and as long as the girls appeared comfortable, Allison's CASA training told her that their sharing of memories was a healthy form of expression.

"If you don't mind my asking," Shane's voice was light, "are you babysitting these two?"

Allison didn't want to get into specifics but also didn't want to arouse suspicion of what she was doing with two children who weren't biologically hers. She decided on the simplest explanation. "I'm their CASA volunteer. Do you know what that is?"

"I've heard of it."

"I'm helping out the Westmorelands, who are their foster parents." Allison wasn't about to crack open the girls' histories, even if she was tempted to use their foster status to inquire again about the possibility of a no-fee pavilion birthday party rental again. Perhaps she could ask him later, away from the girls. She wanted to keep their activity focused on their water recreation. But to do that, there was something she needed to know.

Now.

"How do you steer this thing?" There wasn't anything that looked like a steering wheel or gearshift.

"Let me show you." Shane adjusted his knees to ease his feet from the pedals. "Keep your side going."

Allison pumped her feet in a steady rhythm, and the boat started to careen to the left. "Uh-oh." She suddenly felt off balance.

"It's okay," Shane coached. "When you apply more pressure to one side, the boat turns that way."

Allison shifted in her seat and tested things by pumping with a bit more gusto. "I see." The boat made a smooth, donut-shaped turn.

The girls threw their hands in the air, eating it up. "Do that again!"

But Shane jumped in with an offer. "My turn."

"You want to give it a try?"

"Sure." He cracked his knuckles and then flexed his arms. "I always wanted to be a boat captain."

"Really?"

"I'm absolutely kidding about that. These legs are made for land."

"We'll get you back there soon enough." Allison couldn't help but notice how she was shoulder to shoulder with Shane, acting like partners on what was supposed to be a simple outing with the twins.

But the ease at which she interacted with him and, in turn, he with all of them, surprised her.

In a good way.

Allison turned the helm over to him, and he completed two turns in the opposite direction.

She was feeling cheeky. "Nice job, Showboat."

He teased her back. "I've got a few more tricks up my sleeve."

"Let's see." She cast a sidelong glance.

"Coming right up." He paused just long enough for the

boat to halt its movement atop the water. "I'll need your help with this one."

Allison was ready to oblige.

"If we both pedal backward, let's see what happens."

Allison joined Shane in more teamwork maneuvering, which took the boat into smooth reverse. Doing so put the girls in the view of the driver's seat.

"I like this," Olivia apprised.

"Me, too," agreed Isla. "I can see everything this way."

Allison laughed. "How long do you think we can keep this up?" She looked to Shane.

"Until we hit shore."

Allison could keep pedaling for that long—and then some.

Shane's presence was comforting. His relaxed posture and warm voice put Allison at ease and made the girls smile. He was making Allison smile, too.

"So how many boat rides have you taken so far?"

"This—" he turned to look at her, his words as tender as his tone "—is my very first one."

"Seriously?" Allison blanched.

"It's the truth."

On second thought, it made sense to Allison, too. It wasn't likely the staff played bumper boats in the water after their shifts or went for joyrides on their lunch hour.

Suddenly, Allison remembered the brown paper sack she had seen Shane carrying. "Did we interrupt your lunch break?"

He waved a hand in dismissal. "Don't worry about it."

Allison's cheeks flooded with heat as she apologized. "I'm so sorry. I never intended—"

"I know." Shane wouldn't let her go any further. "It's no big deal. Really." Then, flashing a megawatt smile that shone as bright as a Texas sunset, he insisted, "I'm enjoying this."

Something about those last words settled onto Allison like hot stones during a back massage, a little awkward at first but then subtly soothing.

Because she was enjoying herself, too. Not just the girls' company, but Shane's, in a way she couldn't have predicted.

The pedal boat coasted to the bank, beaching itself with ease. Shane pumped the pedals one final time to propel the boat just forward enough that he could disembark on dry land and not get his boots wet.

He hopped out of the boat. "Thanks for the taxi ride," he joked to the twins.

They delighted in his humor. "That will be five dollars, please." Isla held out her hand while Olivia snickered.

Theatrically, he reached into his back pocket, slid out his wallet, pretended to find what he was looking for—and then paid the girls in high fives.

"Awww." Olivia's face was a mixture of jubilation and disappointment. "I thought we were really going to get five dollars."

"Okay, Olivia." Allison worked to redirect her attention. "Are you and Isla ready to go out again? Just us girls?"

They both answered with a loud "Yes!"

"Should one of them be moved to the front with me?"

"It'll be okay," Shane assured her. "Now that you've gotten the hang of pedaling, you'll be fine out there."

"Won't I just go around and around in left turns?"

Shane shook his head. "I'll shove the boat back, and you can pedal to steer it into the water. Then just ease up when you need to turn, and let the wind adjust the boat when it needs it."

"I think round two is going to be a little slower for us."

"Slow isn't a bad speed."

Allison cleared her throat as if to say something, then stopped.

Shane quickly changed the subject. "Be sure to stay in your seats, girls."

"We will," they promised.

Shane's heart softened at their replies. They were too cute for words.

He gave a final reminder of how to land the boat when they were ready. "Just like we did earlier. Give the pedal a final brisk kick, and that will drive the boat up the slope and onto dry land."

"Will do."

"Then just leave it parked far enough on the bank so it doesn't get carried back out again. You can use this rope if you need it." He held up a soggy end that was tied to the front.

"Got it." Allison flashed a thumbs-up sign. He waved them on their way, the girls using both hands to do so as if they had already become fast friends.

He unbuckled his life jacket, slipped out of it and then marched it back to the storage shed. He was able to keep an eye on Allison and the girls for just a few moments longer as he did. Her ponytail swung from side to side in the breeze, and her wide smile could be seen by him all the way from the water's edge, letting him know she was doing just fine.

She was a quick learner. And one tough cookie, Shane thought to himself as he glimpsed the twins for a final time on the pedal boat they seemed to be enjoying more than any carnival ride.

Making memories didn't take much. Just time, effort and a little willingness to experiment.

Shane tucked away that reminder as he followed the trail back to the headquarters.

* * *

"Troy called from Big Bend Park." Nadine handed Shane a Post-it with a phone number scrawled on it as he entered the headquarters.

"Thanks." Shane recognized it as his friend's cell number. "I'll give him a call in my office."

Shane was always happy to talk with his longtime buddy, who was stationed as a ranger at Big Bend Ranch State Park, a mecca of a state park that occupied over 300,000 acres in Texas from the Rio Grande bordering Mexico into the canyons and backcountry of the Chihuahuan Desert. While other parts of the state were becoming crowded, far-flung west Texas still had plenty of open space.

"Hey, Troy." Shane was glad he picked up on the first ring. "What's up?"

"Just checking on you. How's Cottonwood Creek?"

"So far, so good. Although it's a bit early to tell."

"Staff okay?"

"For sure. Two other rangers here help split the duties. Good guys." Both rangers were on the younger side of their careers, which helped Shane feel more comfortable in his interim management role. "What about you? How's everything out there?"

"That's why I'm calling." Troy paused. "I know it's still early for you with getting settled there and all, but have you thought any more about Big Bend?"

Shane blew out a breath. "Every day." It was an honest answer to a deeper question.

When Shane was in high school, he had borrowed his father's copy of Elmer Kelton's classic Texas novel *The Time It Never Rained*. The well-worn paperback was far and away the biggest book Shane had ever tried to read. It didn't take long for him to get hooked, but it wasn't just on the rural storyline.

He was fascinated by the west Texas setting.

"You know west Texas is where I want to be." He yearned for the wide-open spaces far from cities, the high plains which comingled with rugged plateaus beneath blue skies that melted into the horizon. Shane could see them clearly in his mind's eye. At night, twinkling stars blanketed obsidian skies, and people still stepped outside to see them. Those picturesque scenes had cemented themselves in Shane's mind long ago.

"When you can't be a cowboy, you might as well be a ranger in the west."

"Amen," Shane agreed.

"So how's the project-planning coming?" Troy asked.

"It's…" Shane stared at the file cabinet opposite his desk. "Early."

"Do you have a project idea? Because you know that's what the higher-ups want to see."

Shane knew that to move up—and to move west—he needed to show successful implementation of a project that could help his management skills shine while also being something he could leverage in his application to Big Bend.

"You gotta make inroads," Troy urged.

"I'm working on it." But maybe Shane needed to work faster.

"The job you wanted to apply for here should open for applications the later part of June," Troy said. "I'll keep you posted."

"Thanks." It was good to have friends like Troy who could look out for him.

"I hope to see you out here soon."

"Me, too." Shane said goodbye to his friend, thinking

about Texas. Shane's life had started in the east, and he was halfway west with his appointment in Cottonwood Creek. He just needed to put in his time in hopes that his application would eventually be accepted to where he really wanted to be.

Now he needed a project.

Stowing his phone away in his shirt pocket, Shane decided to perform some quick research in one of the dusty file drawers of the back office. He slid open a creaky metal drawer and thumbed through stacks of manila envelopes, each full of printouts and projects that spanned years before his arrival at Cottonwood Creek. Pages of project after project, some yellowing with age.

Since its inception, the park had hosted nonprofit organizations, community fundraisers, high school groups and special holiday events. Some seemed to be recurring, like a Habitat for Humanity spring auction and outdoor dinner. It looked like there were six good years of that.

Shane wasn't interested in necessarily resurrecting a past project, but perhaps he could get inspiration from the files. He pinched the edge of an aging photograph between his fingers, holding it at eye level. It was a photo of elementary school–age kids.

That took him back.

His childhood wasn't as happy as the faces of those in the photograph suggested.

Shane's parents never had what they wanted: more children.

Shane was his parents' only biological child. He grew up in a bedroom flanked by two other bedrooms that were originally for siblings who never were born. Instead, his mom and dad became foster parents, and all kinds of children came and went through their home.

The kids never stayed long. But because there always seemed to be so many of them in the house, it didn't take much for him to feel like an outsider in his own home.

The sour memories still rubbed Shane raw. They had a way of creeping up on him, and he had tried for years to keep them at bay.

He studied the photograph, turning over possibilities in his mind. He needed a project that got more people through the gates of the park. When he took the interim position, he was told to focus on children's programming.

And that was his Achilles' heel.

He had only a half-baked idea about what needed to happen in less than four months' time. But someone with institutional memory might be able to help. "Nadine?" He poked his head around the corner. "Can you come in here, please?"

Nadine took a seat across from him.

"How much do you know about CASA?" Shane clarified, "The advocacy group?"

"Allison's a part of it."

That was why Shane was bringing it up. "Is she an organizer for the area?"

"I don't know."

That was no help.

But Nadine did offer something that was. "They have some of their meetings at the Cottonwood Creek Community Church parish hall."

Shane tilted his head to the side. He hadn't been on church grounds much as an adult. He was more of a lapsed attendee, especially through college and moving around so much as a park ranger. But there was no reason he couldn't set foot there, especially because a program was already starting to form in his head.

"Is CASA county-wide?"

"Do I look like Google?" Nadine cut her eyes at him.

Shane held up his hands in mock horror. "I thought you know everything."

"Use your fancy phone for that." She flicked her hand in the direction of his shirt pocket. "Besides, why are you so interested in CASA all of a sudden?"

Partnering with a nonprofit organization that benefited the community sounded like a win-win.

Nadine's mouth curved. "Or are you interested in that woman—"

"Oh, please." Shane tried to sound as nonchalant as possible.

"All I know is that my new boss—my *single* new boss," she underscored, "just happens to want to know more about a cute runner who loves this park and also just so happens to be single, too."

"And I see someone is trying to play matchmaker."

Nadine drew back. "You young people! Call it what you want, but since you're interested in Allison—"

"For the purposes of a park project."

"Is that what the kids call it nowadays?" She grinned, giving him a side-eye.

Shane brought his hand to his forehead and rubbed the worry lines that he felt forming. Nadine's sassy attitude was one Shane hadn't completely figured out just yet. Still, as long as they worked together, he'd have to put up with her meddlesome habits.

He tried again. "I want to talk to her about something related to the park."

"I see stars in your eyes," she teased. "You're interested."

"I'm interested in doing my job. Nothing more." Shane shut down her matchmaking attempt before she had a chance to say more.

Sure, Allison was attractive. She was fit, enjoyed the outdoors and had a big heart. And she was kind to animals and humans alike.

But he had no time for romance.

He had taken the appointment in Cottonwood Creek to show park system supervisors that he was ready for the next step. And in doing so, he would use his time here to manage a special project that would build his résumé and impress the powers that be. Ultimately, they were the ones who could promote him to the bigger job opportunity out west, which would also come with better pay.

Nadine gave a loud *hmmph*. "Sounds to me like you're cooking up something."

"Nothing yet." At least nothing that had a clear shape. Shane needed time to research and ponder the logistics. He couldn't waste too much of it, though, considering his appointment in Cottonwood Creek had an expiration date.

But there might just be a way to partner with CASA and mobilize their existing volunteer base so he wouldn't have to reinvent the wheel.

Still, there were lots of questions and no answers.

He glanced out the window toward the lake. He couldn't see Allison and the girls, but he knew they had to come back to the headquarters to drop off their life jackets.

He'd need help. He could ask Nadine a few more questions, but she wasn't well-informed about specifics. He needed someone who was.

He needed to talk to Allison.

Because she might very well be the one holding his ticket to a new life in west Texas.

Chapter Four

As Allison and the girls walked back to park headquarters, they did so with a spring in their step. The young girls' smiles stretched as far as the horizon line. "That was awesome!" Isla pumped her fist into the air.

"The best!" Olivia echoed.

"So you two are ready to be boat captains now?" Allison joked.

"For real!" Every word out of Isla's mouth was brimming with enthusiasm, and the same was true for Olivia. The twins gave double of everything, all the time. After a successful pedal boat adventure, it was double the appreciation.

"You're the best, Allison." Olivia took a wide step toward Allison as they walked, wrapping her arms around her waist in a tight bear hug.

Allison slowed down to savor the moment, her heart melting at such an earnest gesture. "Thank you." She shifted the three life jackets she was carrying to one side of her body before bringing Isla in for a hug, too. "You both were excellent navigators."

Olivia pulled back slightly, looking to Allison with the signature same brown hair, innocent eyes and charming cheek dimples she shared with her sister as they continued walking. "Shane taught us everything."

"He's really cool," Isla said, falling into step next to her identical sister. "And I think he liked us."

"You're easy to like." Allison couldn't let the opportunity for a natural compliment pass the girls by. "You both are." They needed extra praise and these small shows of affection as much as any young girls, but even more so because of their circumstances.

"So are you." Olivia smiled up at her. "And Shane thinks so, too."

This conversation had suddenly veered in a direction Allison wasn't expecting. "Why do you say that?"

"Because he was smiling at you."

That wasn't how Shane had acted around her at all.

Was it?

Allison picked up speed to keep pace with the girls so that they didn't run too far ahead. As she walked, she replayed the boat ride in her mind.

Shane had smiled.

But they all had.

He did sit close to her.

But that was by design. The boat seats left little choice.

No, the girls' imaginations were running wild. Because Shane wasn't interested in her. That would be utterly ridiculous.

Allison shook her head, trying to cast off the thoughts. She was giving far too much credence to them. They weren't serious. They weren't even true. They were simply part of the girls' overactive imaginations.

Nothing more.

As they approached the Cottonwood Creek Park headquarters, Nadine slid the window and waved to the girls. "Did you all have a good time?" she asked.

Squeals of delight were followed by exuberant banter back

and forth from the girls. Nadine's wide smile at the happy report from the twins made Allison smile, too.

"Looks like today was a success." Nadine's gaze rose to Allison where she stood behind the girls.

"I'll say." Allison had to agree with Olivia and Isla. She held up the jackets. "These came in handy. Thank you for them."

"Let me get Shane." She pivoted on her stool and called for him before Allison could intervene. "Shane! Got some life jackets for the shed."

"I'm sorry. If I'd known I should have returned them by the lake, I would have left them near the—"

"No worries." Nadine waved her hand in dismissal, turning back toward the window. "We've got some cleaning and inventory to do tomorrow down there, so Shane might as well just take them now."

"Okay." Allison lowered the life jackets and looked for an area to place them as she pivoted right to left. "Should I put them here or—"

"Right in my hands!" Shane's assured voice rang out as the office door opened and he approached her with open arms.

"Oh, I, um..." She struggled for words as Shane swooped toward her to take the life jackets. His strong forearms flexed as he curled the trio of them into his chest. Allison cleared her throat, trying not to stare.

"Girls, how was the rest of the boat ride?"

"The best!" Once again, they launched into mile-a-minute praise as they recapped their adventure. At one time, Allison remembered the girls being a bit shy around new people, though there was not a shred of that today. The park setting had helped them be themselves and relish in the joy of simply being children.

That was what they needed.

That was what these sweet girls deserved.

And that was exactly why Allison wanted to honor them with an outdoor birthday celebration.

As if reading her mind, Shane said, "You'll have to come back here sometime, maybe for a special occasion." He looked to Allison as the girls did as well.

"Please?" Their eyes begged her to agree to Shane's offer.

"Yes, of course we can come back here." How could Allison resist?

"Great." Shane moved one step closer to Allison, lowering his voice just a tad. "Maybe you and I can talk about an idea I have for a community project here at the park. Something that could help kids like these two—and others as well."

The idea piqued Allison's interest, though the memory of their prior exchange about her facility request for the girls' birthday celebration was still fresh. "Would it involve the pavilion?"

"It could." Shane nodded. "I might have been too quick with my answer to your, um—" his eyes darted to the girls as he simply said "—*request*. The other day?"

"I remember."

"There might be something we could do as part of a larger project."

If Shane was opening the door about her request, she was ready to push the possibility further.

"I'd like your help with something. You're someone in the community who's connected to the needs of others, and that's who I need helping me with upcoming plans. Maybe we could talk more about this, say, one-on-one sometime?"

"Oooooh!" Olivia's eyes lit up in surprise. Isla made kissing sounds into the air. "We told you he likes you."

"Girls!" Allison chided, feeling her cheeks redden at their insinuation.

Shane looked from the girls to Allison and back again before breaking into a chuckle. The genuine smile that erupted across the park ranger's face did nothing to diminish his masculinity. On the contrary, seeing a rugged ranger navigating the waters of interaction with young children did something to Allison that she couldn't quite put her finger on. It was endearing and alluring but also seemed completely natural, like there was something in Shane's character at the heart of the exchange.

Shane just laughed off their antics and looked to Allison. "So, what do you say?"

To the opportunity that might help her throw these girls a birthday party after all? There was only one answer that Allison could give, and she couldn't say it fast enough.

"Yes."

Shane had wildlife encounters of all varieties through his time as a ranger. Mammals, reptiles, even some ornery park patrons on occasion... Nothing rattled him.

Except the twenty-four-hour aftermath of a surprise scorpion sting.

Nadine insisted he get medical attention when the swelling hadn't reduced in his forearm Thursday.

"It happened at the shed at Cottonwood Creek Lake," he told the front receptionist when he was checking in at the Lone Star Clinic. "Late afternoon yesterday."

"So you've had symptoms for eighteen hours?" She typed as he talked.

"Give or take."

"And you're a new patient?"

Shane nodded.

"Dr. Zambrano does take walk-ins, so if you have a seat, I'll call you as soon as an exam room is free."

"Thank you."

"While you're waiting, will you please fill these out?" The receptionist handed Shane a clipboard of paperwork. While he didn't expect high-tech services in a small town, he expected something a little more modern.

Then again, it wasn't like the Texas State Parks System operated on the cutting edge of technology, either. Maybe some services—like medical ones—were better with an old-fashioned approach.

"Sure." He forced a tight smile before choosing a seat in the small waiting room and settling the clipboard on his lap, answering details of his medical history. Halfway through the first form, though, a wave of something struck, causing his fingers to curl and his arm to seize. He winced, dropping his pencil to the floor.

He breathed through the pain with his eyes closed as an electric shock spread through his arm.

"Are the forms really that painful?" A familiar female voice offered a momentary distraction to the burning sensation that lingered beneath his skin. Shane opened his eyes.

"Allison?" He blinked twice, fighting to keep his wincing at bay.

"What's happening?" She dropped to his side, crouching next to his chair.

"I'm fine."

"You don't look fine."

He tilted his head back and forced his fingers to move. "See? Just a little scorpion bite."

"Ouch." Her posture straightened. "Tingling and numbness?"

"Like you wouldn't believe," he admitted.

"Have you ever gotten stung before?"

"Not like this." Shane didn't want to show her the swelling beneath his long-sleeved shirt. He'd save that for the doctor's assessment. "Do you know the doctor who's taking walk-ins today?"

"Absolutely, Dr. Zambrano. You're going to get great care from her."

Shane withdrew his hand, the tingling subsiding a bit. "Her?"

"Yes." Allison rose to her feet, crossing her arms over her chest. "Do you have a problem with a female doctor?"

Shane shifted in his seat. "I never said anything about that."

"From your reaction it looked like—"

"Don't jump to conclusions." Shane tried to keep his voice down, but this sudden turn in their exchange was adding to the discomfort that was already making him edgy.

"Trust me, people come in here with all kinds of preconceived notions and stereotypes." Allison's stance didn't budge. "So if you think—"

"Stop." The word came out more forcefully than Shane intended. "You don't know what I think. I just need someone to look at this, probably tell me I'm okay and send me on my way with maybe a prescription for antibiotics so this doesn't get infected."

"Sounds like you know exactly what you need, then." The hope for any saccharine exchange before he was called back to an exam room had completely evaporated.

"I need to fill out these papers." He tapped the edge of the clipboard. "So if you could be so kind as to—" he pointed to the pencil that had fallen to the floor and was now resting next to Allison's shoe "—hand that to me, please?"

Allison uncrossed her arms, bent to retrieve the pencil and

gave it to Shane. "I hope you feel better soon." Then, without another word, she turned on her heel and disappeared through a doorway near the receptionist area.

While seeing a familiar face was nice, having their simple conversation turn south was not what he expected. The awkward exchange with Allison made him question how easy it would be to work with her when, just a day earlier, the possibility had seemed so promising.

Like the whip of a scorpion's tail, his feelings now swung in a different direction. Partnering with a Cottonwood Creek local may not have been Shane's best idea.

Chapter Five

Allison collapsed into the office chair of her cubicle.

She didn't regularly interact with patients in the waiting room, but on her way back from a supply closet, she had detoured through there and saw Shane.

And now she wished she hadn't.

What was up with him? Was he on edge because of the scorpion sting? Or was it because of her?

Trying to pin down emotions had never been Allison's strong suit. In her last relationship, her ex had complained about her communication skills. It was either too much, too little, or just plain complicated. Her boyfriend's preference for how he wanted her to act shifted based on the day of the week, and while she really enjoyed his company and some of the interests they had in common, they were two very different people.

That was always a hard relationship pill to swallow.

At least that rural doctor-in-training whom she thought might be Mr. Right wasn't someone she had to see at work anymore. He had finished his time at the clinic and was back in Galveston to finish the rest of his schooling, enjoying Gulf Coast living that was a world away from her small-town life in Cottonwood Creek.

Allison wanted someone steady in her life, but finding

exactly the right person was something she was still figuring out. Her encounter with Shane underscored how out of practice she was when it came to communicating clearly with a member of the opposite sex.

Had she overreacted with Shane? What had he said, exactly?

Perhaps she had cut him off. But since there was no way to rewind the past ten minutes, all she could do was look forward. And, right now, looking forward involved invoice creation, data entry and lots of digital accounting.

At least that was something Allison could handle.

"Hey there." Her coworker Juleah nosed her way over the side of her cubicle as Allison was finishing a quick report. "I need your help with something."

"Sure." Allison's fingers paused on her keyboard. "What's up?"

"I need you to look into a patient's bill from two months back. Medicare was supposed to cover it, but she's insisting we sent her an invoice for a visit."

"Who's the patient?"

Juleah shared the name. "She's waiting in the lobby."

Allison didn't want to go back out there, especially after her botched encounter with Shane. "Want to send her back here to me?"

"I shouldn't. She's got knee problems, and she's waiting for a ride from her daughter. I told her I'd check with you about it."

"That's nice of you."

"No biggie." Juleah shrugged. "It gives me a chance to ask about your plans for the night."

"Plans?" Allison continued navigating her screen as she asked, "What plans?"

"Bingo." Juleah snapped her fingers. "Allison, you're twenty-four, and you need to get out more. Have a little fun."

"I get out." She went running, spent time with the twins, went to church, saw her mom on Sunday afternoons...

"You know what I mean."

Allison did.

"Why don't you join me and some of the girls at The Starlight tonight?"

"I haven't been to that music hall in months. Ever since—"

"I know." Juleah held up a hand. "You don't have to explain about he-who-shall-not-be-mentioned."

"Thank you." Allison was genuinely relieved when her coworkers, whom she considered friends like Juleah, had rallied to her side after the breakup, not judging or rubbing failure in her face. Her only sister, Jessica, was attending college out of state, and while she offered encouragement at a distance, nothing could replace the support coming from real people in her everyday life.

"Annie and the Hill Country Howlers are playing. Monica and Kaitlyn are coming." They were two nursing aides who worked at the clinic, both in their twenties like Allison. "Monica's sister is probably going to join us, too."

Allison was good friends with her, and since she hadn't seen Evie in a couple of weeks, that tipped the scales. "Sold. I'll come."

"Terrific! Live music on a Thursday should help us get through the end of the week here."

"I'm all for that. But," Allison insisted, "I won't dance."

"Who said anything about dancing? Just some friends, having a relaxing time listening to some good music."

That did sound nice.

Allison found exactly what Juleah needed and printed off

a document for her to take to the patient, glad to cross one item off her to-do list.

"Meet us around seven thirty?"

"I'll be there," she promised, looking forward to the girls' night.

***

"Let's have a look." Dr. Zambrano leaned forward, taking Shane's arm in her hands. "Can you tell me what happened?"

Shane relayed the details about being in the shed at the park when he felt a strong sensation hit. "The sting was intense. I knew exactly what it was."

"Did you see the scorpion?"

"Saw it," Shane confirmed. "And killed it. Under these very boots." He looked down at his feet.

Dr. Zambrano rotated his forearm right to left. "It's a scorpion sting all right." She gave him a sympathetic look before lowering his arm and patting his hand. "But I sense you might have a pretty high tolerance for pain. Am I right about that?"

"Depends on the day of the week." Shane rolled down his shirtsleeve as he spoke.

"You didn't come in yesterday."

"I didn't think I needed help yesterday."

"Fair enough." There was no judgment in Dr. Zambrano's voice. What was probably two decades of medical experience helped her deliver words simply and calmly. "May I just get a quick listen to your heart?" She reached for her stethoscope on the counter as Shane nodded, sitting up straight as he inhaled and exhaled at her command. "Good." She removed the ear tips of the stethoscope. "Considering your earlier vitals and the medical history you shared—" she nodded to the clipboard the held the forms Shane completed "—I have no reason to believe this is going to get any worse." She shared some additional facts about stings, allergies and existing condition considerations. "But that doesn't apply to you. So I'm going to prescribe something for immediate relief, just to get you over the hurdle of today and to help in the coming days."

"That would be much appreciated." Shane had a full slate of responsibilities at the park, and he didn't need anything to slow him down.

"Now, if you don't see an improvement with the site pain or if you develop any further tingling or any intense numbness or a persistent ache, I want you to call me."

"Here at the clinic?"

"No." Dr. Zambrano reached into the pocket of her lab coat. "This number goes direct to our answering service, day or night. A real human answers the phone, and that person will put you in touch with me."

Shane accepted the card, swallowing his surprise at being able to have such personal medical support a mere phone call away. "That's more than I expected."

"You haven't had a primary care doctor you could call in the past?"

Shane had to answer honestly. "No."

"Well..." She curled the stethoscope and replaced it gently on the counter. "You're in Cottonwood Creek now. People around here care about one another. And as long as you're a patient of this clinic," Dr. Zambrano assured him, "you'll have somebody caring about you."

Shane had anticipated a medical exam, but hadn't bargained for a bit of personal PR about his new home.

Temporary home, he reminded himself.

"Thank you." Shane put the card in his shirt pocket. What the clinic may have lacked in the latest technology, it made up for in bedside manner and care from the people who worked there. And in that small, unexpected way, the place he was in started to feel just a little bit like a home.

Annie and the Hill Country Howlers' song lyrics were stuck in Allison's head all the next day.

Thursday night had been exactly what she needed. Early European settlers of Texas who built the rustic, all-wooden Starlight Music Hall at the edge of town couldn't have known the generations of locals it would entertain.

It had stood the test of time, and was now a charming live music venue that showcased local talent as well as larger bands that sometimes drew big crowds. Twinkling lights that hung from rafter beams above the spacious dance floor gave the space a festive atmosphere. Comfortable, inviting tables on the periphery begged people to stay awhile. And that was exactly what Allison, Juleah, Monica, Kaitlyn and Evie had done. They soaked up the sounds of the band, savored carne asada tacos and lots of guacamole, and enjoyed one another's company as they pushed their cares aside for a night.

At one point, she swore that she saw a familiar park ranger. While from a distance it looked like it might be Shane, it turned out to be his fellow ranger, Lucas.

Shane was clearly still on her mind.

Lucas had swung by the group of women, talked for a bit and then moved on with his own group of friends. Still, seeing him made Allison think of Shane, and that was when she said a silent prayer that his doctor's appointment had gone well and that nothing else had happened to make his scorpion sting worse.

In hindsight, she did feel bad with how she left things in the waiting room: he was new to the area, it was his first time in the clinic and he was in pain. She could have handled that interaction better than she did.

While she couldn't address anything with Shane now, she certainly knew where to find him.

She had earmarked time in her schedule for a late-afternoon run after work, and if she encountered Shane, she vowed to ask him in person how he was feeling.

If that had a positive outcome, then she also vowed to ask more firmly about the pavilion use so she could move forward with the party plans for Olivia and Isla. And this time, she wouldn't take no for an answer.

She hummed a few more lyrics from the band she'd heard the other night to get her through the day. At the end of it, she traded the music in her head for earbuds and her exercise playlist as her feet pounded the trails at the park.

It was May in Texas, one of the state's prettiest months. Spring rains gave way to gorgeous new plants as hope blossomed throughout the landscape. The evidence was everywhere, from the smallest of buds to the largest trees. The trails of Cottonwood Creek State Park provided an especially attractive showcase each year.

But before the namesake trees of the park spread their cottony fluff, other vegetation announced their arrival into the spring season. Mountain laurel exploded with vibrant purple blossoms, turning the evergreen shrubs into colorful showstoppers along the park trails. Native wildflowers emerged in fresh, vivid blooms. Bluebonnets were the most noticeable, with their telltale shade, but other colors adorned verbena, wine cups and bee balm.

Allison inhaled the deep fragrance that saturated the air as she ran along her favorite trail, casting off the responsibilities of her workday.

Focusing her attention on the trails helped.

As her body found its rhythm, things that had previously bothered Allison melted away.

Now, if she could just bottle this feeling. As she approached the zigzagging switchback trails, she took each curve with cool confidence. She wasn't trying to win a race. She was simply trying to push her body to appropriate limits and maintain an active lifestyle. The back-and-forth pattern of switchback running was some of her favorite stretches along the trail. For her, movement was meditation.

Cresting the last curve, she maintained her momentum and strode the final straightaway that led back to park headquarters.

The trails never disappointed.

And, hopefully, neither would the conversation she planned to have with Shane. He had opened the door of possibility to her use of the pavilion free of charge, but after their exchange at the clinic, she might have blown it. She needed to smooth things over...for the twins' sakes.

Because they deserved a special birthday celebration.

The absence of their biological parents should not stop them from making memories. Happy times still needed to be a part of their lives.

They were children, after all.

Allison exhaled deeply as she slowed her pace to a steady walk. She used the last portion of the trail to catch her breath and complete a post-exercise cooldown.

She darted into the park restroom, splashed some water on her face and retied her ponytail. Nadine had informed her that Shane and one of the other rangers were tied up with something when she inquired. Because of that, Shane was going to meet her at one of the picnic tables outside the park headquarters to chat after her run. Allison was relieved that he was back at work after his appointment yesterday, and she said a quick thanks to God for that healing.

When she exited to find Shane, it didn't take her long to

see him. The handsome ranger was standing next to one of the tables under a grove of trees, talking into his cell phone. In his crisp uniform with badge, name tag and utility belt, he looked every bit the picture of authority: tall, commanding and self-assured. Yet, there was also something approachable about him.

He was as comfortable in a pedal boat as he was along park trails. He helped women, and bantered with children. Ranger Shane Hutton symbolized both leadership and altruism, no small feat for someone his age.

Which appeared to be about Allison's.

Not that such a thing mattered.

But she noticed.

Allison was noticing a lot of things about Shane Hutton as she approached him, including his chiseled jaw, broad chest and the way the late-afternoon sun made his eyes sparkle.

But Allison wasn't there to stare at Shane. She forced herself to rapidly blink as a means to focus on the task at hand, which was business related to the park, not something personal related to the ranger.

Shane waved her over as he finished his phone call, placing his cell phone back into the front pocket of his shirt.

"How are you feeling?" Although Shane looked fine, she wondered just the same.

"On the mend." He straightened his arm, flexing his fingers as he rotated at the elbow to showcase his range of motion. "Tingling is gone. The prescription ointment from Dr. Zambrano was just what I needed."

"My prayers were answered." Allison blew out a breath.

"You—" Shane rested his hand on his utility belt "—prayed for me?"

"Yes."

"Oh." Shane looked down. "That's…um…" His eyes rose

to meet hers. "Really appreciated." Were his cheeks turning a bit pink?

"It's the least I could do. I also needed to ask for forgiveness," Allison said. "I'm sorry for jumping to conclusions yesterday. I didn't let you finish talking when you were in the waiting room, and it was wrong of me to make an assumption."

"Thank you." Shane's gaze softened. "I wasn't my most pleasant self, under the circumstances. By the way," Shane added, "I really liked Dr. Zambrano. She has great bedside manner and was super efficient."

Allison definitely agreed with that. "She's the best. Quality medical care in a rural area is such a blessing."

"I was grateful to have it. Thank you for being a part of it. And," Shane said, smiling, "thank you for checking on me in the waiting room. As far as anything that happened between us there, it's water under the bridge. Truly."

Allison's guilt settled, and she suddenly felt self-conscious. It wasn't just from being in her workout clothes.

Still, Shane had a way of putting her at ease, in spite of what she was wearing or what had happened yesterday.

"How was your run?"

Allison was happy to focus on something else as she shared some stats. "It's nothing to brag about. But I always like being able to get the miles in here at the park."

"It's a great place to exercise. I wish more people would take advantage."

"Me, too." Not that Allison wanted the trails overrun, but she did want people to enjoy this gem of a place that was in the community's very backyard. "More people need to experience the outdoors here."

"That's exactly what I wanted to talk to you about." He gestured to the picnic table. "Have a seat?"

"Sure." She slid onto the bench seat of one side as Shane took the side opposite her.

"When we were at the lake, you told me you're involved with CASA."

"Yes. For several months now."

He nodded. "And the girls?"

"The twins are my first case."

"How large is the CASA system in the area?"

"That depends on what part you're asking about. The volunteers?"

"Yes. We'll start there."

The number changed month to month, but at any given time, there was a strong core group. Allison answered, "There are about two dozen adults here in the county who serve as special advocates for the children in the system."

Shane retrieved a slim notepad from his shirt pocket along with a ballpoint pen. He clicked the pen's top and scribbled notes as he continued. "And the number of children they serve?"

"That's hard to pinpoint. Active cases right now—" Allison thought for a moment "—are about that many. I'd say two dozen. But, again, that changes."

"Sure."

"Are you interested in volunteering?"

"Not exactly." Shane put his pen down. "But I do have an idea to help the children."

Allison straightened her back. "Here?"

"Right here." Shane's own posture firmed as he gestured over the side of his shoulder. "Actually, over there." He pointed in a vague direction to the location that Allison had her eye on for the girls.

"The pavilion?"

"Bingo." He flashed a thumbs-up sign as he clicked his

tongue, a cute gesture that made Allison sense a playfulness about him. She knew he had a fun side. He was, after all, someone who willingly killed time doing donuts in a pedal boat with her and two young kids. But on the chance that such an experience was a one-off event, she wasn't sure of the true nature of Shane Hutton.

"I want to give the CASA kids—and the volunteers—a party."

"A party?" Was she hearing him right?

"Well, maybe a party." He hemmed through his words. "Or a picnic. A play day. A jamboree. Whatever we want to call it."

"We?" She raised her eyebrows. "I mean, I'm excited. Don't get me wrong." Her mind raced through images of Olivia and Isla enjoying the type of birthday they never before had, with double the enthusiasm and double the memories. "But is this just for the twins?"

"It's for everyone. The organization is a nonprofit, right?"

"Of course."

"Between the volunteers, the directors, the kids, even the court officials, this could be a great opportunity to give everyone the chance to sort of relax for the day. But more than that, if local businesses get involved with, say, food, beverages and maybe even some activities, we could turn this into something more than just an appreciation event."

"We could turn this into a celebration." Allison spoke the words like a mantra, the possibilities running through her mind faster than she could capture each one.

"Exactly!" Shane's enthusiasm rang forth like the notes in a song.

Allison wasn't about to let the momentum stop, and this was her in. "The girls are having a birthday."

"I remember you mentioning that." Shane asked, "When is that?"

"June third. They'll be six years old."

"That's just two weeks away."

"Right."

"So, wait a minute." Shane's posture changed. "You're the one spearheading the party for them?"

Now it was Allison's turn to be playful. "Bingo!" She echoed Shane's word from earlier and mirrored his thumbs-up gesture, which made him crack a smile. "Look, Olivia and Isla are sweet girls."

"They are."

"They're living in a foster home. Their lives have been completely turned upside down due to no fault of their own." She felt herself choking up at even these vague references to their struggles. "All I want to do is help them feel like every other kid, you know?" Allison swallowed hard, the weight of challenges they shouldn't have to shoulder feeling heavy.

Shane's face registered the severity of what she communicated. "I understand." His voice dropped an octave. "Really, I do." His eye contact and something about his tone struck Allison. Shane wasn't just sympathetic. There was another layer to his reaction.

Something personal.

Allison chose her words carefully. "I'm glad. Because when it comes to these girls—" she fought a rising lump in her throat "—they are important to me. They deserve better than what life has given them."

"I can understand that." Shane didn't flinch. "Trust me."

"I do." The quiet words escaped as Allison held Shane's gaze. The moment seized both of them without warning, as strong as a spiritual moment.

Something had happened.

An admission, and a feeling.

And as Allison sat across from this man, she kept her eyes locked into his, not wanting to break the feeling, even for the briefest of moments.

Chapter Six

Shane was not a party planner.

He was comfortable with big-picture plans when it came to the running of a large state park but not the details of individual planning. That was why parks had staff members like Nadine. The park needed someone with her skills to help with all the small-picture items. But for a new project like the one Shane envisioned, he needed more than Nadine. He needed someone outside the office who had her pulse on the local community and who could get the work done.

To pull off what Shane was wanting would take teamwork. Allison certainly seemed like a team player.

"How about doing this on a Saturday?" Shane asked.

"Saturdays are perfect."

"Late morning or early afternoon would draw the most people."

"It could definitely stretch between those times," Allison offered, her eyes widening as she spoke about the possibilities.

Her enthusiasm was contagious. It fueled Shane's momentum as details took hold. As they talked, Shane felt himself getting pulled in her direction because there was something about Allison...

Confidence and self-assurance were attractive traits to

him. He wanted those things for himself as well. After all, if he could attach his name to a successful project at Cottonwood Creek State Park, then he'd fill a hole in his résumé that had kept him from his true goal of advancing further in the state park system.

And going west.

Shane had twice been passed over for promotions to larger parks because of his lack of experience. The state park system of Texas was a hierarchy: smaller parks got the newest rangers, the ones with fresh badges who could cut their teeth on manageable lands. There were plenty of small parks in the dense forests of east Texas.

But Texas was bigger than those assignments, and so was Shane's ambition.

West Texas parks were meccas of the old west spirit. Hundreds of acres were under the umbrella of each one there, as opposed to much smaller plots in east and central Texas.

There was nothing wrong with these smaller park systems where he had worked. They had neat offerings, and people certainly benefited from marked trails and informative displays along with picnic areas and parking lot access. They liked having restrooms and gift shops.

Pavilions and pedal boats like those in Cottonwood Creek catered to day users. But parks in west Texas were destinations. People camped, explored and stayed awhile. Being there for a length of time was a restorative experience.

Maybe Shane needed some restoration for himself as much as the people who visited those places.

Shane wasn't about to be passed over again, though, the next time he applied for advancement. If he was to be taken seriously as a contender for appointment to a west Texas park, he needed to improve his résumé.

Four months is all it would take.

That time would go by faster with someone like Allison to help him with this idea. As she talked more about CASA, Shane started forming additional details and found himself getting behind the mission of the group. To hear Allison talk about all they did, the volunteers were doing important work.

"So you want to throw a CASA party?" Allison's words held a touch of skepticism. "Why?"

"I know a little about the court system and the needs that kids have." That part was true, but Shane wasn't about to go into his family's full past with Allison. "It's terrible to think about what they lose."

Allison's face softened. "Absolutely."

Shane held up a single finger. "For just one magical day, I'd like to be able to help kids like Olivia and Isla forget their past and focus on their present."

"You remembered their names." Allison's voice was breathless, a note of gratitude ringing through her words.

"Of course I did," Shane said, smiling. "I loved meeting them. And I loved spending time with all three of you." At that admission, his heart skipped a beat, which he hadn't expected. It took him a moment to gather himself to continue. "Look, all I have is this park." He gestured around him. "I can't bend the rules for a private party for the twins. But I can still make some kind of party happen if we use this angle."

"You're finding a way to help them." Her words weren't a question, though Shane suspected she had a few.

"I can provide the pavilion if it's a community event. I can label it an outreach, and then Nadine won't fuss about the rental paperwork. Neither will the administrative powers that be who are above me. But I need more than Nadine's help." He repositioned his feet beneath the table. "I need yours."

Allison brought her hand to her chest, inhaling a breath. "You've already gotten me excited about this."

Shane felt that, too, but in more of a personal way than she probably did. But now was no time to entertain feelings. He shifted himself back to the task at hand. "Your boots are on the ground here. You know Cottonwood Creek—its people, its needs—better than I do."

"Give yourself a little more credit." Allison dropped her hand and placed it on the table between them. "You know this place pretty well yourself."

"I'm learning." Shane leaned forward. "But I could still use a local's help."

"And that's where I come in?"

If this event was really going to happen, Shane needed not only Allison's local connections, but her swift help as well. "June third, you said?"

Allison nodded. "Yes, that's the day of the girls' birthday. It actually falls on the first Saturday in June this year."

"Then let's make the event happen for that day. The park will bill it as a CASA appreciation event, but you can privately bring whatever you want in for those girls."

"Like party favors? And cake?"

"Most definitely cake." Shane smiled, as much at the thought of a yummy pastry treat as well as the knowledge that this idea was taking flight. "What's a party without cake?"

In one swift motion, Allison grabbed both his hands in a burst of gratitude that surprised Shane. She squealed, "Thank you!" It all happened so fast that the intimacy of it hit him with hurricane force.

Though like strong winds, the moment was felt—and then it passed.

Allison pulled back as quickly as she had reached out to him. "There's so much to prepare!" she said.

When was the last time he had held hands with a woman?

Or been embraced by one? Shane's mind raced with past questions as well as future ones.

Allison unzipped a side pocket on her running shorts and reached for her phone, clicking the side and swiping the screen. It gave Shane a moment to compose himself. "I can start making a list." She started typing with one finger.

There was no place to entertain feelings at the moment, so Shane shelved them. He started this all, and he needed to make sure to only ask the questions that related to their plan. "Can you help with the outreach?"

"Most definitely." Allison's brunette ponytail bobbed with her nod, a cute and confident expression blooming across her face.

"I have some general funds that can be used for food and supplies, but I'll have to be lean. Can you help me find the best local catering as well as some decorations?"

"Sweet Swirl Bakery will help us out. Penny, the owner, keeps everything very reasonably priced."

"I like the sound of that."

"That's where I had planned to get a birthday cake for the girls. But Penny can also make sandwich, fruit and cookie platters to order, and she can probably throw in some complimentary paper products. The cost of things like that add up."

Shane was well aware of budgets that could get out of hand. He had seen some missteps in places where he previously worked, and he didn't want to make any of those himself. Park officials throughout the years had preached watchful eyes when it came to spending.

"Helium balloons don't cost much, but they make a big impact. Especially for kids. They can even take them home after the party."

"Great idea." This kind of knowledge was exactly why Allison was so valuable. He wanted to tell her so, but he worried that personal comments were too likely to derail him. Plus, he had a few more questions about the logistics. "What about gift bags for the volunteers and the kids?"

"The clinic where I work would love to get involved with this." Her voice lifted in enthusiasm. "I'm sure of it."

"Promotional stuff?" Shane was all for giveaways, though he didn't want to make this too business-centric.

"We've got some cute kids' stuff that I can round up. Medical vendors are always giving the clinic things, and you'd be surprised how many items are sitting on a shelf in our storage closet. Stuffed animals, fidget spinners, these cool flashlights with a clip on one end..."

"Those things actually sound perfect." Shane wasn't about to back out of this idea now. "Maybe there are even some other avenues you can think of—"

"I'm on it." Allison's confidence was contagious. "Look, for a community event, the possibilities open up so much. People in Cottonwood Creek are generous, and they'll be itching for an opportunity like this to share what they can."

"Do you think they'll attend in an actual show of support?" Because, ultimately, bodies through the park gates is what this event needed to produce.

"I *know* they will." Allison's words were as believable as the reality that was taking shape.

Which Shane was starting to like very much.

Very much indeed.

And he wasn't the only one who noticed.

After they punched in their numbers to each other's phones and said goodbye, Shane went back into the park headquarters office. Nadine gave him a long side-eye. "Exchanging numbers with Allison, I see?" It wasn't so much a question as a nosy observation.

"I'm sure you could see everything from inside here."

Nadine gave him a knowing look. "I saw the two of you getting close."

Shane stayed in business mode. "There's a community event the first Saturday in June that the park is going to host. Allison is going to help, so we need to be in contact."

"First I'm hearing of this." Nadine crossed her arms over her chest.

"We've got a lot to talk about."

"Oh?" Nadine pursed her lips. "You and me? Or—" she paused and raised an eyebrow "—you and Allison?"

The sound of them as a couple—even from the lips of nosy Nadine—made Shane's chest tighten. His heart was already reacting to thoughts and feelings that he was having a hard time catching. Sorting those in front of Nadine wouldn't work. "Listen, I'll tell you everything you need to know after I make a phone call." He stepped toward his office at the back of the small building.

Shane opened the door to the one actual office inside the headquarters, a semiprivate space where he could close the door and have a moment to himself. Because after that exchange with Allison, he needed one.

That woman did something to him.

Her energy.

Her enthusiasm.

The touch of her soft hands—if only for the briefest of moments—made him melt inside in a way he hadn't anticipated.

Maybe Cottonwood Creek was softening this park ranger.

Or maybe it was just Allison Van Horn.

When Allison got her first phone message from Shane, she was at work on Monday. She saw it when she reached into her purse for lip balm and noticed the notification on her screen.

Shane thanked Allison for their Friday talk, gave a bulleted update of his progress so far with the party planning, then ended with a funny meme that made Allison chuckle.

Appreciation, organization and humor; she could definitely work with this guy.

She typed out a quick reply, letting him know the progress she had made as well with catering plans and the decorations over the weekend. She also let him know she'd be approaching Dr. Zambrano about some donations at the end of the day. Quickly, she searched for an equally entertaining meme to send back and settled on a cartoonish one that she hoped would bring a smile.

She tried to savor this initial back-and-forth that already felt comfortable and cooperative. Shane made things easy.

If only everything around her could feel the same way.

She stowed her phone, swiped on some lip balm and turned her attention back to her desk.

Her workweek was starting off with a couple of complicated billing snafus, and Allison was trying to untangle them all. She had already run some reports, and sitting with the printouts, she was going line by line to compare insurance adjustments and patient out-of-pocket expenses.

Allison was good at problem solving, and she'd get to the bottom of these inquiries. She just needed to follow the trail of paperwork, data input and receipts to find her answers.

She also needed a few answers from Shane.

Reaching once more for her phone, she typed Invitations? because that was one aspect of the upcoming park event they hadn't discussed. Who was going to be invited and how they would receive the outreach had yet to be determined.

Been thinking about this, Shane texted back. Can we talk over dinner at The Valley Steakhouse tonight? My treat.

A weird feeling moved through her stomach, and it wasn't just the thought of a rib eye that caused it.

Dinner with Shane?

That sounded suspiciously like a date to Allison.

And she wasn't quite sure how she felt about that...

Chapter Seven

Shane looked at himself in the mirror. It felt good to shed his park ranger uniform and wear something more casual. He finished buttoning his crisp, light blue button-down shirt.

Grabbing his wallet from the counter and his cowboy boots by the door, he readied for his dinner with Allison.

Nadine had sung the praises of The Valley Steakhouse, and her recommendation wasn't the only one he had heard. Since being in Cottonwood Creek, he was learning there were places that were high on locals' lists, and this longtime institution was one of them.

But Nadine didn't know Shane was meeting Allison there tonight. No one did.

That was what Shane wanted. No need for prying eyes to show up or curious gossipers like Nadine to start speculating. This was a dinner, but it wasn't a date. Shane needed to iron out specifics regarding the upcoming park event, and texting with Allison could only go so far. Plus, he wanted Allison's opinion on several things that needed immediate attention, and he also knew he was asking her to take on a lot in a short amount of time. The least he could do was buy her dinner to show his appreciation.

He pulled up to the steakhouse in his red Ford pickup, the tires crunching against the gravel parking lot. Large, centuries-old oak trees framed the wooden building where patrons were greeted by a long porch that could probably tell a hundred stories. The welcoming entrance was flanked by rocking chairs and several hanging baskets of bright bougainvillea. Their magenta flowers and bright green leaves popped against the steakhouse's rustic exterior that, while looking original, was still well maintained with a nod to classic country craftsmanship.

Shane arrived earlier than their seven o'clock reservation. Though it was a Monday, he wasn't sure how crowded this place might get, and certainly didn't want to keep Allison waiting alone.

No gentleman did that to a woman.

Shane was seated by a hostess who must have been highschool age. She took his drink order, and he also got water for both Allison and himself. Their waters and his sweet iced tea were brought in glass Mason jars. "Perfect," he said, then thanked the hostess and hefted the glass, feeling its substantial weight in his hand.

The heart of Texas might not be officially the South by some arbitrary standards, but all of the Lone Star State sure knew how to satisfy when it came to embracing Southern comforts like refreshing beverages and good drinkware.

"No sweet tea for me?" Allison teased as she came up behind Shane, greeting him with an easy smile when he turned to welcome her.

"Hi there." He swiftly put down his glass and stood up. "Let me get your chair." Shane helped her into the wooden high-back that matched his at their table.

Her mouth fell open ever so slightly at his quick gesture. "Thank you." She brushed back a strand of hair from her face as she made herself comfortable. A light, fruity scent of something sweet teased Shane's nose. He wanted to ask what perfume it was, but tamped down the words before he could verbalize them.

This wasn't a date. And he shouldn't be acting like it was.

"Thank you for meeting me here," he said. "I took a chance in selecting it."

"You can't go wrong in Cottonwood Creek. There's not a bad restaurant here."

"That's good to know." He took his seat again. "I forgot to ask before I offered this place, but I hope you're not a vegetarian."

"Most decidedly not." Allison unfolded her napkin and placed it in her lap. "That's a sin in Cottonwood Creek." She winked, putting Shane even more at ease.

"I'm certainly learning the ways here."

"You're getting quite a crash course."

Shane's slightly sweaty palms came as a surprise, but once he and Allison shared this first laugh, they fell into an easy rhythm of conversation that made it seem like they were old friends. The waitress took their orders, and before she left to go, Shane added, "One more sweet tea, please."

Allison leaned forward once the server disappeared. "It's really the only way to drink tea, am I right?"

"I'll say. I was practically raised on it. From the cradle to the grave."

Allison smiled at that. "Was that in east Texas? Where you were raised?"

"Yes." Shane nodded. "About twenty miles outside of Huntsville."

"Which direction?" Allison showed a real interest in everything Shane said as their conversation continued, with him revealing a few details about his upbringing and his life before Cottonwood Creek that he hadn't even intended to share before he stopped abruptly. "You know, I didn't actually ask you here to talk about myself."

"I know. You brought me here for the tea," she teased. Then she raised her glass, and Shane met hers in the air, smiling at her deftness both in steering a conversation and being in tune to what made other people comfortable.

They clinked their Mason jars before Shane reminded her, "We do need to talk about the CASA event."

"Of course we do." Allison put down her glass. "We've got to get this off the ground fast to be ready for June third."

"My thoughts exactly." And before their food arrived, they were already brainstorming logistics related to invitations and outreach.

"But we need a clever name for this. It can't just be a CASA celebration."

"We need to brand this?" Marketing was a bit outside Shane's wheelhouse.

"We need to *sell* this," Allison corrected. "Cottonwood Creek residents have a lot of competition for their time. But I've already looked at the Chamber of Commerce website and checked a few online community boards."

Shane hadn't even thought to look into what else might be happening during that same weekend in and around the area. "And?"

"We're in the clear."

Shane blew out a breath.

"Luckily for us, Memorial Day weekend events and high school graduation festivities are going to be in everyone's rearview mirror by the time this event happens. The CASA kids, their advocates, our area foster parents, the court staff, new volunteers…" She spoke with assuredness and confidence. "Everyone should be free to come."

Shane liked the sound of that. "So what's going to get them here? What catchy name do you have in mind for this?"

"Let's brainstorm." Allison extended her hands onto the table, using the space to gesture. "On the one hand, this is a Saturday event, so we could make it something alliterative." She scrunched her face in cute consideration. "Social? Shindig? Soiree?" Allison stopped herself. "Am I sounding too much like a thesaurus?"

"Not at all." Shane extended his own hand, meeting hers even though he didn't mean to do so. "Oh." He pulled back, feeling embarrassed at the contact that seemed to surprise her as well.

"It's okay." Allison folded her hands back into her lap, looking down at them.

"Did I just derail our brainstorming?" he asked, his voice low.

She looked up at him, meeting his eyes and looking into his gaze. Blue eyes as sparkly as Texas topaz seized him, a quiet moment stretching between them in spite of the din of the restaurant.

Just then, the waitress arrived and slid two dinner plates between them. That helped remind them what they were supposed to be doing, which was not getting lost in each other's attention.

The waitress placed succulent rib eyes, steaming mashed potatoes, fresh green beans and buttery yeast rolls in front of them. "This looks delicious," Allison said.

"Please enjoy your meal," the waitress said. "And let me know if there is anything else you need."

"I never eat like this." Allison sat up taller before picking up her knife and fork. "On a Monday, I mean."

"That makes two of us."

As Allison savored her first bite, she announced, "But I certainly could. This is amazing."

Shane started on his steak as well, his table manners as polite as his words. After a few more bites, he asked, "Now, where were we?"

Allison had to backtrack to remember where they left off in their CASA conversation. "We were talking about a name for the event. Something catchy."

"And that's where you come in. You're bound to have a better handle on this than I do."

"When it comes to communication," she was choosing her words carefully, "it's best to be direct."

"I agree." Shane's reply dripped with a double meaning that Allison decided not to address. If she did, this dinner would turn even more personal, and she wasn't ready to handle that. Not with commitments to Olivia and Isla hanging in the balance. They were her priority in all of this.

"So let's keep that clarity in mind with this event."

"You won't get an argument from me there," Shane added, "But I do like your alliteration angle."

"Then let's try that." Allison offered one more idea. "How about calling it The Saturday Stroll to benefit CASA?"

Shane swiped at his mouth with his napkin as he finished a bite, pondering it a bit before exclaiming, "The Saturday Stroll? I love it!"

"It implies the outdoors and sounds inviting, right?"

"Yes, and that's important. The name will make people think of something leisurely and comfortable, which is exactly how I want locals to view the park. That way, they can come to the grounds, feel welcomed and stay awhile. The Stroll communicates that."

Allison agreed. The rest of the dinner passed with more back-and-forth detail sharing. "The CASA volunteers meet at Cottonwood Creek Community Church. It's where I attend weekly services. I think it would be nice if you came to the next meeting."

Shane's posture stiffened. "I don't know..."

"We don't meet in the church itself," she clarified. "We just use the parish hall."

Shane took a long drink from his tea. "When's the meeting?"

"This Thursday night."

The tenseness in Shane's shoulders softened.

"It would go a long way to making people feel invested in this event." Allison placed her utensils down. "You wouldn't have to stay for the whole meeting. There are announcements at the beginning, so if you come at six thirty, I can introduce you and then send you on your way. What do you think?"

Shane's posture relaxed further. "I'm in."

It was refreshing to have a project come together so fast. Allison was grateful to move toward a shared goal with someone so easily.

Once their meals were finished and the waitress had cleared their plates from the table, Shane's gaze returned to full focus on Allison. His undivided attention should have made her nervous, but instead it made her feel like she was glowing. She and Shane had successfully brainstormed all they needed to get this event going.

"Thank you for joining me tonight and being on board with this." Shane slid the check the waitress had placed at the edge of the table his direction. "It means a lot."

"My pleasure," Allison replied. "You know, this is going to mean the world to those girls."

"You really care for them, don't you?"

"I do." The twins were so easy to love. "You've met them."

Allison's memories of their sweet pedal boat ride played like scenes of a movie in her mind.

"I have." Shane reached for his cell phone. "And I have the picture to prove it."

"Wait—what?" Allison blinked back surprise as he scrolled to a photo of her and the twins silhouetted against a gloriously blue Texas sky on the day of their lake adventure at Cottonwood Creek Park. "You took this when we were on the pedal boat?"

"I couldn't resist." Shane tilted the phone back to himself to get another look. "It's beautiful. The whole experience you created for them that afternoon was as well."

Allison's heart melted not only from his compliment but also from his desire to capture such a tender moment. "Those girls." Allison sighed. "How can your heart not go out to them?"

"You're a person who leads with her heart," he said, leaning forward. "I sense that."

Allison hoped her cheeks weren't flushing. "That's fair to say."

"That's an admirable quality."

These veiled compliments were filling her up more than a luscious dessert, which she was glad they weren't sharing. That would have made this feel even more like a date.

Which it wasn't. She reminded herself of that.

Still, their cooperation, their give-and-take and now this shared photograph were sealing something between them. It was a sweetness that was palpable. So why shouldn't Shane enjoy some of that, too? Her words toward him came from a place of sincerity. "I sense that about you, too."

"Oh?" Shane's right eyebrow arched playfully.

This ranger was smooth as well as handsome. And Allison needed to be careful not to get distracted by that. Still, she couldn't help reciprocating because from the way Shane worked in service at the park to the caring gestures he had extended to the twins, his actions had already spoken loudly to Allison. "Your heart seems big as well."

But a larger question loomed. Was that big heart of Shane's available? Entertaining that question took Allison by surprise because she couldn't have anticipated this when she agreed to meet Shane for dinner.

Yet, here she was, not only asking that question in her mind but also asking a more important one about Shane's obvious big heart that involved her.

Did Allison want it to be?

Chapter Eight

"Look at what we taught Lucky to do!" Isla held one end of a jump rope while Olivia grabbed the other. They stretched the rope between them, then inched toward the puppy, his right ear flopping over his eye as he looked from girl to girl and back again.

"Are you ready, Lucky?" Olivia counted to three, and on her command, she and her twin slid the rope against the grass as Lucky bounded over it.

"We taught him to skip rope!" The girls nearly collapsed in giggles before they both yelled, "Again!" Lucky obliged with puppy dog skips as the girls worked to maneuver the rope under him. "See? He's such a good boy."

"He is a good boy." Allison had to admit that the girls' trick was cute. "Now, if you can get him to double Dutch, I'll really be impressed."

Isla's eyes spread wide. "What's that?" Before she knew it, Allison was explaining the technique and thinking back to her own childhood.

"I've got another rope." Olivia raced into the garage and came back hoisting a second jump rope in the air. Allison couldn't help but beam. Leave it to the girls to accept a challenge.

"Okay." She took a seat on the lawn, the backyard's plush

grass cushioning her. "Let's see what Lucky can do." The girls had fun attempting to alternate the ropes, although Lucky was now more interested in trying to grab them in his mouth for a game of tug-of-war.

Late spring days in Texas stretched into the evening, with dusk falling well after dinnertime. That gave Allison more time after work to do as she liked. She regularly ran at the park, but this Tuesday she was forgoing exercise in order to spend time with the girls, which was important so that she could be a good advocate for them when it came to court proceedings, complex and ever shifting as they were. Allison had gotten a crash course on the legal system herself through CASA trainings but then had learned even more through her assignment to the girls' case. While the girls didn't need to appear in person at every legal turn, their voice needed to be there, and that was where Allison came in. Allison wanted the twins to have everything they deserved.

Mia and Michael were providing a safe environment, and through interaction with their other children and enrollment in school for the first time, the girls' lives were already enriched. But with school ending for summer break soon, the kids were going to have more changes. Mia was a stay-at-home mom, so thankfully there would be consistent care for them. But the girls could never have too much love from others, including Allison.

Maybe love was a strong word, but their bonds had formed quickly. Allison did love these girls, and she was committed to helping them thrive by supporting them in school, giving them outlets for play and being a role model to them.

Seeing the fun the twins were having with such simple objects reminded Allison to ask Dr. Zambrano about donating a few promotional items stored at the clinic for The Saturday Stroll gift bags along with other items she would be rounding up for June third. "Girls." She gestured for them both to join her. "Come here a moment, please."

Each found a way toward Allison, Lucky in tow. They collapsed onto the grass next to her, Lucky chewing on one rope like it was the most interesting thing in the world. "Yes, Miss Allison?" Olivia said, looking to Allison with puppy dog eyes of her own.

"I wanted to talk to you about your birthday." Allison had already spoken to Mia and Michael, and now she could share the good news with the girls.

"We'll be six!" Isla exclaimed, flexing her fingers with five on one hand and one on the other. "See?"

"Yes." Allison mirrored her movement. "You're both getting so big."

"I feel taller." Olivia sat up a little straighter.

"No, you're not."

"Am too."

"Girls!" Allison cut in to their conversation before more bickering could happen. "About your birthday." She put her hands on her knees. "I want to do something really special."

"Because we'll be six?" Isla asked, every word, like their movements, full of exuberance.

"Yes." And because, Allison privately thought, these girls have never had a celebration. "It's a big deal to be six and to be finishing kindergarten."

"We love kindergarten," Olivia interjected, and Isla nodded her agreement.

"So think of this as a summer celebration for kindergarten and also your birthday." Allison kept her voice full of pep. "Let me tell you what we're going to do."

Olivia and Isla leaned forward in excitement, absorbing every word that Allison shared about the plans she had made, the park, the pavilion. "There will be cake," she promised.

"Chocolate?"

"Yummy vanilla?"

"Icing, too?"

"With sprinkles?"

The girls' questions were as rapid-fire as their enthusiasm. "Yes, yes and yes." Allison wasn't always quick to make promises when she couldn't control the outcome on some things, but this was one commitment she had already handled. Penny at Sweet Swirl Bakery had already promised a combination flavor cake, and a friend at church had shared some leftover decorations. Candles for the girls to blow out would be the only thing she would still need to buy for the event.

"Now I need you to do something for me, okay?"

"What, Miss Allison?" Isla put her petite hand on Allison's knee.

"You've got to be on your best behavior. You'll be six years old, after all." Allison wanted to set boundaries so the girls knew what to expect. "There are going to be a lot of people there. Some people you'll know, like everybody in this house. Me, of course. And then the park ranger."

"The one who came with us on the boat? Mr. Shane?" Olivia clapped her hands again, this time in front of her.

"You remember him?"

"He was so nice!" Isla joined in on the compliment that Allison hadn't expected.

"Yes," Allison agreed. "He's very nice." Her mind flashed to their dinner two nights ago, which had been the best start to her workweek in recent memory. She also remembered the sweet photograph on Shane's phone, and her heart softened toward him even more. But the butterflies in her stomach at the mere mention of him were something she needed to ignore in order to stay focused. "And he has an important job at the park to keep everyone safe. So that's what I wanted to talk to you about." Allison looked from one girl to the next. "There will be no running off to the lake. We'll be at the pavilion, so—"

"What's a pa-billion?" Olivia tried hard to mimic Allison's word.

Isla reached for Lucky, settling him onto her lap. He relaxed into her hold, soaking up the attention.

"It's an outdoor building, kind of like a really big porch." Explaining something new to a child always took extra effort, but Allison was finding her way. "That's where we're going to have the party. And it will be a lot of fun. So—" she looked each girl in the eye "—can I count on you?"

"We'll be good!"

"We promise!"

The girls beamed at Allison.

How could she not adore these two?

She stayed with the girls another half hour in the backyard, soaking up time with them as well as the last few rays of the day's sunshine. Then she ushered them inside, spending a bit of time talking with Mia in the kitchen and saying hello to the other children before she wished everyone a good night and drove back to her house.

When she fished her phone from her purse to charge it for the night, she had a voice message from Shane. Earlier in the day, she had sent him a reminder about the CASA meeting at the church's multipurpose room on Thursday, along with a digital map pin of the location. Since he was still new to Cottonwood Creek, she didn't want to take a chance that he might get lost.

But in the message, that possibility flew right out the window. He offered to pick her up so they could drive to the meeting together.

First the boat ride.

Then Monday's dinner.

And now Thursday's meeting.

She was spending more time with Shane Hutton than she would have ever guessed.

But she wasn't complaining.

Hearing from him and knowing they were working toward the same goals brought as much comfort to her as what she would have expected from a romantic relationship, which she kept having to remind herself that she wasn't in—though, if she had her way, she might have to take matters into her own hands after The Saturday Stroll and entertain the possibility.

"Sometimes I think these supplies rearrange themselves." Dr. Zambrano pointed at the shelves in the clinic's supply closet that held everything from printer cartridges to tourniquets.

"I haven't been in here in ages." Allison looked around at the other shelves. "Is this where you keep most of the promotional items?"

"Among other things. Let's have a look." Dr. Zambrano started scanning the shelves on one side while Allison tackled the other. Allison really enjoyed working for Dr. Zambrano, and it was a rare occurrence during the busy workday when they got to interact one-on-one.

"Here's what I was looking for." She gestured to a stack of blue gift bags and several cardboard boxes on the top row. "Those are filled with freebies for The Saturday Stroll you told me about. In addition to keychain flashlights, stuffed animal toys and some really neat fidget spinners, there are some beautiful hardcover children's books. At least two dozen. They were left over from an elementary outreach program we had several years back."

"That's very generous." All the CASA kids at the event were going to love having that as part of their goodie bags. "They sound perfect."

"Oh," Dr. Zambrano said, pointing to one additional box. "There are some travel hand sanitizers, branded with the clinic's logo. You can include those for the adults."

"I can't thank you enough."

"I'm glad they're going to a good cause. Help yourself, and just make sure Anita inventories them when you take them out the front door at the end of today."

"Of course." Given everything that Dr. Zambrano had just shared, Allison wanted to be overly transparent with what was leaving the clinic, and the office manager Anita was the right person to keep track of that.

"Great." Dr. Zambrano cut the lights of the closet as she stepped outside it, Allison following suit. "Take some photos of the kids with their goodies. And the volunteers, too. Sounds like you can make some great gift bags for everyone."

"Yes," Allison agreed, especially with the way everything was shaping up so quickly for The Stroll. "And don't forget that you're invited. The email invitations are going out tomorrow, but I wanted you to know that you would be most welcome." Allison added cheerily, "Free food and cake that day!"

Dr. Zambrano offered a warm smile and a pleasant decline. "June third is already booked for me, but thank you, Allison. CASA is very lucky to have you as a volunteer."

"I appreciate that very much." Allison admired Dr. Zambrano on so many levels, so to receive an earnest compliment from her that not only spoke to Allison's character but also aligned with her passion for volunteerism meant a great deal.

Later, after Anita helped her inventory everything and carry two cardboard boxes to her car, she decided to detour to the park on her way home. She kept clean workout clothes and an extra pair of running shoes in her trunk especially for occasions like this, when the weather was too tempting to resist. She'd change out of her work attire in the park's restroom, and at least log a few miles before tackling the assembly of the goodie bags at home that evening.

"Good afternoon, Nadine." Allison waved.

"Taking advantage of this gorgeous weather today, Allison?" Nadine waved back.

"Yes, ma'am," she responded. "Can I use the restroom to change?"

"Be my guest." Nadine took Allison's park pass card to scan before passing it back to her. Allison then made her way into the front office, winding her way to the restrooms near the back. As she pivoted to turn into them, she nearly collided with a certain park ranger she knew.

"Oh! Shane, I didn't expect you."

"Nice to see you, Allison." Shane's rich voice was as appealing as it was on the phone message she listened to more than once the night before, but it was even better in person. "And like this."

Allison looked down at her work attire.

"I guess we both have uniforms." He smiled before adding, "Reminds me of what a hard worker you are."

"I stay busy." Allison's gaze darted from his face to the restroom door and back again, eager to get on the trails. "Just changing into my running clothes."

"Of course." He took a small step backward. "Don't let me keep you."

Around Shane, she seemed to lose just a bit of her reserve, going with the flow no matter where things were leading them.

"I'll let you get to it, then." Shane gestured his hand in a sweeping flourish as he comically stepped aside, the ranger taking another step back as Allison walked past him.

She swore she felt his eyes on her as she did, a feeling that she quite liked, if she was being honest.

Once out on the trails, Allison's feet struck the packed dirt with precision.

Putting one foot in front of the other was simply satisfying, especially in shaking off that impromptu exchange with Shane. The last time she experienced such feelings were with that resident doctor-in-training six months ago. That short relationship started strong but fizzled. Plus, he'd been finishing up his commitment to the clinic the very week he had finally been bold enough to ask Allison to meet his parents. He'd thought their relationship was moving in one direction when it was actually moving in the other.

Once he moved back to Galveston, their long-distance relationship was too challenging, especially since they'd never really addressed communication issues and fully gotten their connection off the ground. They parted amicably enough, but Allison was left with a bit of regret. She was twenty-four years old and still single. Plenty of her friends were either in committed relationships or, like Mia, were happily married with children. Was something like that in her future? And, if it was, when might Allison start to feel like those goals were actually possible?

She contemplated her personal life as she kept running. When she committed romantically to a partner, she would be like her mother—all in—not running from responsibilities like her father.

As she crested the top of a small hill, she powered through the incline, stopping only when she reached a partially shady spot where late-afternoon breezes greeted her. She rewarded herself with deep breaths, filling her lungs with fresh oxygen as she basked in her runner's high.

She tapped her smartwatch, storing her stats for later as she strode back to the front of the park, sipping from her water bottle as part of her cool-down routine.

When she arrived at the entrance, Shane was exiting the building. "Allison!" he called, holding up his hand. "Glad I caught you." He smiled sheepishly. "Again."

She smiled and took another sip of water.

"About tomorrow night." Shane widened his stance, his muscular shoulders and ample forearms on full display as he crossed them casually in front of him. "I had asked you about going to the CASA meeting together."

"Yes." The message he left was on replay now in her mind as it dawned on her. "Wait, did I never answer your message from last night?" Allison realized that while she certainly had done so in her mind, she never did in real life. "I'm so sorry." She brought a hand to her slightly sweaty forehead.

"You're busy," Shane offered. "I get it." While it was nice of him to say so, there was still plenty of time and space—and manners—left for her to return a call.

"I didn't purposefully ignore your message. Not in the least," Allison underscored, stopping short of saying something like, *I played it multiple times just to hear your attractive voice over and over.* "Yes," she quickly corrected. "We can attend the meeting together, if you don't mind staying for the duration. It shouldn't be more than an hour, really."

"Not at all," Shane assured her.

"So it's settled." Allison was glad to have that cleared up.

"Not quite."

"Oh?" Allison felt her forehead wrinkle.

His undivided attention was still focused on her, quickening her heartbeat in spite of the cool-down portion of her exercise routine.

"My pickup truck won't drive itself," Shane said, though Allison was still confused by those words. He added, "I need to know where you live."

And just like that, her heartbeat picked up more than at the height of her workout. Shane Hutton did something to her that even a run in the park couldn't sort.

Chapter Nine

Days were all about balance.

Shane was trying hard to achieve that. On a daily basis, he dealt with plenty of park business that needed his attention, from overseeing maintenance and upkeep as well as visitor assistance and information. But there was office work as well, from computer input to reporting, permitting and registrations. Of course, Nadine helped with much of the paper pushing, but he was still in charge of a great deal.

Coming to Cottonwood Creek was a crash course in doing it all. And that was exactly what he needed at this point of his career.

As a professional, Shane was drawn to becoming a ranger because of his love of the outdoors. And while he didn't necessarily enjoy the monotony of administrative tasks that kept him behind a desk at times, he knew it was necessary in order to do what he loved, which was showcase the beauty of Texas and help others experience that, too.

That was how he was approaching The Saturday Stroll to benefit CASA. Logistics and planning weren't his favorite tasks, but he would do his part in order to ensure that the goal of getting more patrons through the park gates and—hopefully—converting them into paid pass members happened in the end. That was, of course, aside from the community outreach aspect that was simply a good thing to do.

Plus, he had Allison to help him.

She was a force of good, and it was easy to work with her. There was a camaraderie that was quick to develop between the two, made easier considering she was enjoyable to be around.

And attractive to look at.

That was why the surprise of running into her yesterday had hit Shane so hard.

He'd have to tamp down those feelings and keep his attention on the task at hand, which was very decidedly not starting a relationship with Allison Van Horn, tempting as that may be. He was leaving Cottonwood Creek soon.

He hoped.

A step toward that was The Saturday Stroll. But before he could add this feather in his cap to his application for Big Bend Ranch State Park, he had to focus on CASA. He needed to find the courage inside him to fully face this event, hard as it was to do because of his past. Memories of his childhood came rushing back.

Those bedrooms for children never born.

The revolving door of his household making him feel like he was never enough.

His parents' divided attention.

He would never make the missteps they did; this he swore to himself. With a prestigious park appointment in west Texas, he could finally prove to himself—and them—that he was worthy of this assignment as well as larger responsibilities and, ultimately, of their respect. But he could also put comfortable distance between them so he wouldn't continue to be reminded of the hurt from the past.

That was where maintaining balance played a role. He'd

get the ultimate chance at that tonight. But he'd also have Allison by his side, which would keep his attention from drifting to the past. He had the present to focus on, after all.

He had just enough time between leaving the park and returning home to switch out of his gear and uniform and change into regular clothes. Wrangler jeans. Cowboy boots. A classic pearl snap shirt.

He was a Texan through and through.

After climbing into his red Ford pickup, he headed to Allison's home using the address she had given him. She lived on a quiet cul-de-sac not far from the center of town, in a row of duplexes that were well-kept with plenty of available street parking. The neighborhood looked as friendly as she was.

He squinted to read the numbers on the homes. Hers was the second to last on the street, with a window box of colorful blooms beneath a single window. The short walkway was lined on the sides with rocks for xeriscaping, a landscape technique that eliminated the need for irrigation. Fresh water had long been Texas's most precious resource, so Shane appreciated when people took it upon themselves to conserve.

Shane parked, jumped down from his truck and advanced up the walkway to Allison's front door. She answered after the first knock. "You're punctual," she said by way of greeting when she opened the door.

"I am a man of my word." He stepped back from the doorway, giving her room to step outside, lock the door and join him on the walkway. She was dressed casually but smartly, in a pair of cropped jeans and a striped cotton T-shirt, effortless and cool. "This is different than your clinic clothes or your running gear."

"Different...?" She turned to him after she secured the door.

"Not bad different. You look good in everything." Allison's cheeks reddened, and he wished he could have taken the words back. He really didn't intend to flirt with her, but compliments just came so effortlessly around this woman.

"You're not so bad yourself." She managed to flip the script his way. "A man in uniform is great and all, but one who can cut loose is even better."

He smiled at that, walking next to her as they made their way to his truck. "I don't know if I'd exactly call myself a cut-loose kind of guy."

"I guess we'll see," she replied coyly.

Shane lengthened his stride so he could step ahead of her to open the vehicle's door. "Allow me. This side is a bit tricky." It wasn't, but opening a door was still the chivalrous thing to do for a woman, regardless of circumstance.

"Thank you." She brushed past him, a whiff of something sweet floating through the air as she slid into his truck's seat. Her ponytail swayed as she positioned herself, looking totally at ease. That seemed to be Allison in a nutshell: on a boat, on a trail, or in a truck, nothing rattled this woman. So if there were any hiccups at The Saturday Stroll or even tonight's CASA meeting, he had full confidence that she would be in control and that things would turn out fine. Allison was a good person to have on his side.

He walked around the truck and joined her in the cab, bringing the Ford back to life. "Ready?"

"Let's go." She placed her purse on the floorboard and then asked, "How was your day at work?"

"That's always a dangerous question for a ranger."

"Oh?"

"The first day I met you, there was a snake to handle, if you recall."

"Oh, I remember," she said, smiling at him.

He smiled back. "I never know what's going to happen from day to day."

"So what went on today?"

"Today…" Shane leaned back from the steering wheel, stretching as he thought about which of today's micro catastrophes to share. "There was a downed tree on the lower switchbacks, a leak near the overlook's water fountain, fire ants took over the picnic area by the lake, and an activist calling Nadine nonstop on the office line about some online conspiracy theory he had read that had nothing to do with our park."

"That's quite a full day."

"It was totally false, by the way." He added, "That theory."

"And what did Nadine say?"

"I didn't hear all of their conversation, but I know she was firm but fair with the person."

She righted her purse when it toppled on the floorboard around a right-hand turn after a stop sign. "Sounds like you had enough to deal with without the noise of someone just trying to create problems where there aren't any."

"Every day is a busy one." Shane took his eyes from the road briefly to look at Allison. "But a good one."

She smiled back.

He returned his gaze to the road. "How was your day at the clinic?"

She blew out a slow exhale, the loose strands of hair that had fallen from her ponytail lifting with her breath. "Besides stumbling upon some theft?"

"Whoa." Shane clenched the wheel with a firm grip before releasing. "How did that happen?"

Allison shifted in her seat. "There's a patient who was suspected of taking medical supplies on his last visit. He pocketed some syringes and a box of alcohol swabs from the exam room."

"Accidental? Or intentional?"

"That's what we don't know. He's a middle-aged guy, and there wasn't clear proof of anything. But when he came in today, Dr. Zambrano's stethoscope went missing. I saw him coming out of the room, and he looked really suspicious."

"Yikes."

"She got her stethoscope back when she confronted him," Allison added.

"That's bizarre."

Allison went silent. Only after several moments did she respond in a quiet voice, "Do you know why some people make choices like that?"

Shane hadn't expected a conversation between them to turn toward moral decision making, but this was feeling important. "Yes," he answered, before adding, "and no."

"What do you mean?"

"Drawing a clear distinction between right and wrong is easy. Stealing is wrong." Shane thought about the morals he learned growing up. "But when someone's not in their right mind or maybe they're in pain—"

"Yes."

"It can be hard to follow through with what's right and what's wrong. There can be shades of gray."

"The world isn't always black-and-white."

"It would be so much easier if it were, right?"

"For sure."

Shane glanced at Allison, registering the worry that she seemed to carry for this. "When we encounter something like that, it can sometimes be a heavy load to bear."

"I wonder about this patient's family." Allison looked out

the truck's window. "Who does he go home to? Who's looking out for him?"

"Would those answers make a difference in what he did?" Shane wanted to help Allison process this.

"Maybe." Allison turned her gaze back to Shane.

"Humans are fallible," he said. "Not everyone makes the right decisions all the time."

"I don't think this patient saw his actions that way." Allison added, "In fact, I'm sure of it."

"What makes you say that?"

"For starters, if he did, he probably would have apologized and tried to make it right. Instead, from what I heard, he was confrontational."

"I've seen plenty of those instances in my work as a ranger." Shane could write a book about all the park encounters that went sideways.

"So how do you handle situations like that?"

"That's easy," Shane insisted. "You focus on the good."

Instinctively, he reached his hand toward her, placing it on her leg. The supportive gesture was automatic, but it solidified something more that Shane couldn't quite identify because he hadn't been looking for it. The emotion he felt in that moment, however, was pure and genuine.

Allison's palm brushed the top of his hand, a gesture that may have been instinctive on her part, too, but that was no less potent than if it had been planned. If they had been standing, perhaps both their knees would have buckled.

Good thing they were each seated.

Shane let the moment linger between them before their hands separated, hers returning to her lap and his to the wheel. The air inside the cab of the truck felt much warmer than just moments ago.

"I don't ever want to draw a wrong conclusion about a person." As Allison spoke the words, Shane had to tell himself they were referring to the medical clinic's patient and not him.

Not them.

Because there was no *them*. There was only a man, seated next to a woman, trying to help her through a moral quandary. He could accept that role.

"Did talking about this help in any way?"

"Yes. It helped in lots of ways." Her words sounded confident.

Even though she didn't need him to echo anything, he did so to show her he heard what she was saying and that he supported her feelings. "Caring about other people is the right thing to do, even if it's not the easiest thing to do."

"You can say that again. I hate seeing situations like this."

"Especially in a place that's trying to help people like a medical clinic." Shane pulled into the Cottonwood Creek Community Church's parking lot.

"Thank you for understanding that and for listening." Allison's posture seemed to relax even beneath her seat belt. "For some reason, I've been carrying this with me all afternoon. It feels good to have talked about this."

"Give yourself more credit." Shane's admiration for Allison's character grew through this unexpected conversation. He steered the truck into an available space at the edge of the lot. "It takes courage not to judge, and to handle things head-on. It sounds like Dr. Zambrano did that."

"She did. I don't know if I would have handled it with such conviction."

Shane cut the ignition, undid his seat belt and turned toward her. "What did I just say about you?"

Allison did the same and turned toward him. Her dazzling blue eyes locked into his gaze. "You told me to give myself more credit."

"Then believe me."

"We haven't known each other very long."

"Sometimes," he chose his words carefully, "you don't have to know someone for long to understand their character."

Allison paused, but then gave a firm nod.

He hoped Allison didn't feel ill composed. Because after this conversation, he felt a bit on the vulnerable side, too. Opening himself to that was as frightening to him as losing out on the west Texas job. And, if he was honest with himself, maybe more so.

Because being vulnerable with his heart was a much more dangerous proposition.

Chapter Ten

"Before we get to our short child-development workshop for the evening, please allow me to present a special guest." Nancy, the CASA volunteer coordinator, addressed the group of slightly over a dozen individuals, all gathered at the Cottonwood Creek Community Church in the name of child advocacy. "Allison, would you like to introduce our guest?"

"Of course." Allison sat a bit straighter in her chair next to Shane at the round-table setup. "This—" she gestured toward her comrade "—is Shane Hutton, Cottonwood Creek's newest resident and full-time park ranger over at the state park." A round of applause lifted from Allison's introduction. "He's joining us tonight to share with me a special announcement as well as a personal invitation to all of you."

Shane shifted to the front of his seat, giving a quick wave to everyone along with a "Nice to meet you all" greeting as Allison continued.

"On June third at Cottonwood Creek State Park, a CASA advocacy appreciation party and children's picnic will be held. Gates open at their normal time, but the event itself will take place from noon to 3:00 p.m. Come any time you wish, and stay for however long it suits you. This is a way for the community to get to know CASA but also for the kids in your assigned cases to have a chance to enjoy themselves in a safe environment. Parents, foster parents, neighbors, interested future volunteers…" Allison looked around the room, beaming as she said, "Everyone is welcome."

Excited chatter rippled throughout the group, as Shane added, "Park entrance is free that day. We don't want cost to be a barrier to anyone attending. This is our gift to you, the CASA volunteers, who give so generously of your time and talents to this community. So allow the park to give something back to you."

"And there will be goodies!" Allison couldn't forget that important point. "Snacks, drinks and some giveaways for the kids, as well as appreciation gifts to case and court volunteers." More excitement flowed through the group.

"Do you need us to RSVP?" asked one of the women.

"No need," Shane answered. "There will be plenty of space to accommodate everyone." He shared a few more details. Allison's heart expanded not only as she watched Shane but also as she witnessed the reactions from everyone. She called for any questions from the group.

"Just one." Nancy nodded toward Shane. "You come bearing such generous news that I'm wondering how long you plan to be in Cottonwood Creek. Can we count on you as a supporter from this point forward?"

Shane gave a deep sigh, rubbing his hand over his arm as he looked from the volunteers to Allison. "This place has already proven to be very special to me, and I will do everything I can to make the upcoming Saturday Stroll enjoyable for everyone."

The warmth that Allison was feeling just moments earlier cooled a bit. Was it her imagination or did he just sidestep Nancy's question? After their black-and-white talk earlier in the truck, his words here seemed a bit…gray.

She knew his interim position had an expiration date—but

then what? Did he know the exact time frame, or had something else happened with the parks system that he wasn't telling her?

In the absence of any further explanation from Shane, Allison jumped in and said, "I'll turn it back over to you, Nancy."

Nancy then proceeded with the rest of the meeting.

Shane sat firmly in his chair, his attention on the group as Allison leaned toward him and whispered, "Are you okay to stay for the rest of the meeting, even for the child development part?"

"Sounds great to me." Shane settled back into his seat, comfortable as a cloud on a sunny day. He seemed to be soaking up everything in the room.

And Allison noticed reciprocal attention because certain women were soaking him up as well.

There were two teachers from the elementary school as well as Penny's part-time assistant at Sweet Swirl Bakery who gazed toward Shane, letting their eyes linger. Shane had certainly won over this crowd quite quickly.

Though that shouldn't have been much of a surprise to Allison, for Shane had done the same with her.

So why was she suddenly feeling territorial over him? Was she staking her claim on him? Certainly not, because she and Shane were only spending time together because of this project. She needed this event to happen in order to celebrate the twins, and he was a means to accomplishing that. Surely, once The Saturday Stroll was over, Shane's attentions would be over, too.

Wouldn't they?

Allison's hopes had been dashed in the past. Just like so much in her life, she would eventually be left to her own devices, which was fine by her. After all, she'd had a lot of practice with that when her father left. Perhaps that was innately what drew her to CASA volunteerism in the first place—to give others the support that she was once lacking. If she could play a supportive role for children who had a parent who gave up on them like she did, she could help them avoid the feelings of loss and absence that she'd experienced.

Plus, unlike coworkers and friends her age, biological motherhood was not something she was chasing after. When she and her younger sister Jessica played with baby dolls as children, she never felt the instant connection to babies that even her sibling seemed to have, perhaps because Allison had felt the sting of abandonment by their father more fully than Jessica since she had clearer memories of it all. Allison had never grown up with dreams of motherhood for her future. Instead, she knew that she had love to give in other ways, both by being around children through her advocacy service and also at the medical clinic. What she did, in her free time as well as in her professional hours, mattered. She was making a difference for others.

Parents didn't have a monopoly on that. Anyone with love to give could do so. And Allison felt fulfilled by that. She wasn't ready to rock that boat, and she wasn't fooling herself. She absolutely knew the only reason Shane was spending time with her was because of this Saturday Stroll event. She shouldn't try to read into anything because nothing was there.

Fine by her.

After all, with work, the twins and CASA, she didn't have room in her life for a romance.

Right?

Sitting through a child development workshop on church grounds was not on Shane's bingo card for a Thursday evening in Cottonwood Creek. He hadn't been to a church in years.

But taking chances sometimes yielded a win.

The setting was warm and inviting, which made The Saturday Stroll already feel like a success, even though the day hadn't arrived. Just that week, the grounds crew along with Rangers Garrett and Lucas were hard at work at making the pavilion sparkle, and he had Nadine print some additional pamphlets and park pass information to give out to new visitors on the day of the event. Planning for the kids, he had decided to take a cue from one of the other state parks in the system and was working on adapting a nature scavenger hunt for the day. It would be overseen by Garrett and supported by a couple of volunteer park docents. Even the adults could join in, if they wanted.

He thought about all of these things at the CASA community meeting, along with the details he would be adding to his application for the Big Bend Ranch State Park position. That needed to be in by May thirty-first, so he had less than a week to shore that up. Given that date, he wouldn't be able to detail specifics for the success of the event, but he could at least project some of the numbers and itemize some of the outreach. Even being here tonight at the meeting gave him one more résumé line item that he could count as community involvement. Certainly, that would be important for the powers that held the purse strings and the final decision in the interview process.

And speaking of purse strings, he was doing The Saturday Stroll to benefit CASA on a shoestring budget.

Well, he and Allison. Her connections and community know-how were really making that happen. A bonus was that he was making connections tonight with people in the community whom he might not otherwise encounter. Networking was always advantageous, and who knew what Shane and Cottonwood Creek might need in the months ahead?

The CASA partnership had been a good idea. Plus, these CASA volunteers were just so nice, to boot. Nancy had a good sense of humor, peppering in tasteful jokes and funny asides throughout the business portion of the meeting as well as the educational portion that was the focal point. Others seemed genuinely interested in all that was being shared, and there was also a kind of synergy in the room.

People who should otherwise be tired from their workdays and taken from their early-evening responsibilities seemed downright energized by coming here.

Allison was right. The meeting didn't last long, and attending it gave him a better glimpse of day-to-day life here in town. Even listening to facts and tips about child development was more interesting than he thought.

When the event ended and CASA volunteers were mingling and making small talk, Allison deftly worked the room. She smiled easily, she spoke sincerely and her focus made it seem as if every interaction she had was the most important one of the evening.

If she routinely made Olivia and Isla feel like this, too, those twins were lucky kiddos indeed.

"I appreciate your outreach to all of us here." An older man held out his hand to Shane. "I'm Henry."

"It's a pleasure to meet you, Henry." Shane returned his firm grip. "Are you a CASA volunteer?"

"Going on twelve years now."

"Wow, that's quite a history." Shane asked, "How did you get involved?"

"It was a retirement project for me. Something initially that my wife thought would get me out of the house." He winked. "Little did she know it would grow on me."

Shane admired that selflessness. "You must have seen a lot of kids go through the system."

"The first two I helped just graduated high school." Pride shone in the man's eyes. "Good kids."

"Made better by this organization and you, I'm sure."

"I like to think so. It's a good group to be a part of." Henry hooked his thumbs into his belt loops. "Listen, I'll be at The Saturday Stroll, and I wanted to ask if my wife can come, too?"

"Absolutely," Shane insisted. "Family, community, it's what the day is all about."

Henry's head nodded in satisfaction. "Also, we've been meaning to get a park pass. Do you think you could help us out with that?"

"For sure." This was exactly what Shane was hoping for. "We'll get you signed up that day."

"Looking forward to it." He shook Shane's hand again, and thanked him one final time.

"The pleasure was all mine." As Henry stepped away, Shane couldn't help but think about his own father. Maybe it was time for a phone call.

Allison wound her way back to Shane, reaching for her purse and throwing it over her shoulder. "Ready to go?"

After saying their goodbyes, Shane pushed open the door as Allison walked through it, heading back out to the parking lot that was now cast in a gorgeous golden-hour glow. "Would you take a look at that sky!"

"Texas sure knows how to impress sometimes."

"All the time." Bands of dusty pink, bright lavender and a vibrant gold-orange threaded around the disappearing sun, turning the sky into something more Technicolor as the day crept to its close. "This is what I want to see in west Texas."

"West Texas?" Allison stopped.

"I, um…" Shane wanted to corral the words back into his mouth.

"Are you going to west Texas?"

It was an innocent enough question, one that he could have answered a number of ways.

"Or have you been there recently?"

Allison was giving him an out. He didn't have to answer her directly.

Did he?

Now was his chance to untangle himself from the slipup. But as he looked to Allison, he couldn't lie. "My appointment here in Cottonwood Creek is up in early September. After that, I hope to get a job in west Texas." He was going to send in his application this week, but until then, what did he have to share anyway? Besides, the application process often moved very sluggishly in the state parks system, so it wasn't like he'd have an answer about the position anytime soon. "But those things take time."

"Oh." Allison adjusted her purse strap and resumed walking. "Yes, I guess they do."

Shane's footfalls slowed to a step behind her, shame holding him back from walking fully at Allison's side. He wanted to share more of his professional ambitions with her, but he didn't want her to feel abandoned before their project could even happen. He needed her, and there was also a pull to guard her heart from information that might make her question his motivation. Because as much as he wanted the success of this project, he never wanted anyone to feel railroaded by his actions.

Especially someone as kindhearted as Allison Van Horn.

Chapter Eleven

Shane couldn't have asked for better weather the following week when the day of the event arrived.

Refreshing breezes heralded a hearty outdoor welcome as crystal clear blue skies were overhead, not a cloud in sight. The Saturday Stroll was suddenly here, and plenty of people were coming through the entrance of Cottonwood Creek State Park.

Shane was busy, moving briskly from one task to the next, just like everyone else on staff that day.

"You trying to run me ragged today or what?" Nadine snapped. "You know I get paid the same whether I'm busy or idle."

"I like you busy." Shane winked.

Nadine slid the welcome window closed. "Well, I don't. Even with the volunteer docents outside to greet people, all this open-and-close, open-and-close is making me lose the air-conditioning in here. You know how the park system operates," she reminded him. "Pennies count."

"And so do people." Shane tapped the window. "This level of foot traffic is a very good thing."

Nadine made some marks on a Post-it note.

"Please tell me you're actually logging the visitors into the database."

"Don't question my process." Nadine waved Shane away. "I have my system."

"I surrender." He put up both hands and started pacing backward in mock arrest.

"Just let me be. I've got it handled." Nadine always did. Somehow. "Shouldn't you be down at the pavilion anyway?"

"I was just about to head there." Shane wrung his hands before reaching for the headquarters door. "See you later." He pulled his sunglasses into place.

"Try to enjoy yourself." Nadine never minced words. "And be sure to talk with some new people when you're out there."

Shane blanched at the insinuation that he might appear uptight. If anything, after he had finished his west Texas application and hit Send earlier in the week, he was feeling as cool as ever.

Now he just had to wait for news.

And also make this Saturday Stroll a success.

Stepping outside, the sun lit everything in an attractive midday glow. The park was in tip-top shape, and he had a bit of an adrenaline rush at seeing how smoothly everything was operating.

The pavilion was the heart of things. The park's groundskeepers had readied the open-air facility with fresh attention and a brisk cleaning. They staggered the picnic tables and created a semicircle area. Allison and what turned out to be an army of CASA volunteers added all the decorations, including balloons, streamers and a colorful banner that stretched across two pylons to welcome everyone. Speakers played upbeat music, and already attendees were mingling while kids played, with even a few dogs joining in the fun.

"Let's run in the bubbles!" A cheerful voice that Shane recognized as Isla's called to her sister as the two bounded off toward an automatic machine shooting sprays of soap bubbles that floated on the wind.

"Nancy's idea." A voice at Shane's back caused him to pivot.

"Allison, hi!" He pushed his sunglasses atop his forehead as he looked at the woman who had done so much to make The Saturday Stroll happen.

"Some dreams really do come true."

"Are we talking about the bubble machine?" he teased. "Or The Saturday Stroll?"

"All of it." She looked around adoringly, as if taking a mental snapshot of everything. Shane hoped he could siphon even a little of her enthusiasm. After all, it seemed like she possessed an unlimited supply when it came to service and celebrations.

"Doesn't this look great?" Allison's face beamed with pride.

"I wouldn't have expected anything less with you at the helm."

"Us," she corrected.

"Yes, we did do this." Shane smiled. "Together."

She reached for his hand, taking it in hers and giving it a squeeze. "Thank you for this. Thank you on behalf—" she lifted her hand toward the twins "—of them."

He squeezed her hand back before they both loosened the grip, looking toward the two little six-year-olds who had been the reason for all of this. They jumped in and over cascading bubbles, other kids joining in as their giggles spread within earshot, calling others into the fun. One small puppy with a floppy ear even partook. "They look like they're having the time of their lives."

"And it's only just begun."

"You mean this day is going to get better for them?"

"Um..." Allison exchanged a knowing look with him. "There will be cake."

"How could I have forgotten?" Shane playfully snapped his fingers. "Do the girls know that?"

"They know there will be a cake. But they have no idea what it looks like. That's what's so fun."

"They're going to love it."

"Who doesn't? I mean," Allison stressed, "it's cake!"

"Say no more."

"Ladies and gentlemen, we have two very special birthdays in the crowd today." Allison held the pavilion microphone, with two tiaras in her free hand. "Olivia and Isla, will you please join me here?"

Mia held the twins' hands but turned them loose at Allison's call. She was in on the surprise, but the girls' squeals of delight as they raced to Allison told her the secret had never been leaked. "Are those for us?" Isla's eyes were as round as sand dollars, her face full of anticipation. Olivia didn't know what to do with her hands, alternately reaching and pulling away.

"Yes." Allison leaned down in a grand gesture of placing each tiara just so atop their heads that they seemed made for. "You both are as pretty as a princess." The girls delighted in their new accessories as Allison continued speaking to the crowd. "We're all gathered today in the name of supporting others. And these two special little girls need our support today because they have just turned six years old!" A wave of applause and several excited whistles lifted from the crowd. "So please join me in singing a very special happy birthday song to Olivia and Isla." She held up one hand and counted down on her fingers. "Three, two, one—"

"Happy birthday to you!" The crowd of over fifty people—

CASA volunteers, case workers, families, Cottonwood Creek business owners, children, Allison's mom and even the town mayor—joined in a chorus of song that made the girls absolutely giddy. They could hardly keep their feet still, and Allison was having a hard time staying put herself.

This moment was perfect.

On cue, Michael brought out the birthday cake, which was topped with six brightly lit candles. Sweet Swirl Bakery had not let Allison down. Nancy stood in the wings, a matchstick lighter in hand in case the candles needed a redo.

"...happy birthday to yo-ooou!" The crowd finished the last line of the song as Michael stopped before the girls, kneeling down so the cake was at their level. He whispered something to them that no one else could hear.

"Wait, wait!" Isla put a hand against Olivia's chest. "We've got to make a wish."

Olivia nodded. She grabbed Isla's hand, and they both wrinkled their noses in thought before closing their eyes tight and bowing their heads for what may have been a prayer—or maybe just a tight-eyed moment of hope. Then the girls' eyes popped open, their heads shot up and they took a collective deep breath to blow out the candles in one fell swoop.

"We did it!" they cheered.

More applause rose from the crowd before Allison asked, "Who wants cake?"

Two proud six-year-old hands shot in the air, nearly rocking the tiaras off their heads. Of course they would be the first to be served. This was their moment, and this was their first ever birthday party.

Allison hoped these would be memories they would cherish for a lifetime.

Michael rose to his feet, and Mia helped him with serving

utensils, paper plates and plastic forks at the ready. Before long, everyone had a slice, including Shane.

"How is it?" Allison sidled up to him, a plate of her own in hand.

"I've never met a slice of cake I didn't like," Shane teased.

"Good answer." Allison took another moist forkful, savoring the chocolate. "Penny did a great job with the cake."

"No argument from me." Shane leaned a little closer to Allison. "By the way, I have a little something for the twins. I wasn't sure when to give it to them—"

"Aww!" Allison swallowed her bite. "That's so thoughtful!"

"It's nothing much, but it's something I hope they'll enjoy."

"Those girls are grateful for everything." She gestured with her elbow to where they were running in circles, trying their hardest to keep their tiaras balanced. "See?"

"They're grateful for you," Shane declared.

"I don't know about that."

"Give yourself some credit." He took Allison's plate as she finished her final bite of cake, sliding it beneath his own. "They are, even if they don't know how to say so. Just look at them." Olivia had tumbled on the grass, and Isla extended her hand to help her up. "They're as lucky to have you as Cottonwood Creek is."

Allison concentrated on the girls, her cheeks flushing. "Thank you."

"I'm going to throw these away—" Shane held up the plates "—and then can I bring their gifts out from the office?"

"That would be lovely."

"Be right back. Oh..." Shane stopped midstep. "And in about twenty minutes, we'll start up the scavenger hunt, if that's still good with you. Any of the adults who don't want to participate can do the nature stroll instead."

"Perfect. I'll tell a few of the others who just arrived and start rounding everyone up."

The Saturday Stroll was marching along more smoothly than even Allison could have predicted.

"You forget something?" Nadine asked Shane as he entered the park's headquarters.

"I come bearing cake." He held out a paper plate with a corner piece of chocolate cake generously covered in thick chocolate frosting like a peace offering.

"So you do love me." Nadine took the plate from him. "Did you walk back all this way just to bring me this?"

"No."

"Well, you shouldn't have told me that," Nadine deadpanned.

Shane hadn't fully learned what to expect from Nadine, though most days he was getting better. "I have a birthday gift in the office. For the girls."

"You are such a softie."

"I'm not a monster."

Nadine took a bite of cake. "You've got good qualities, even for a boss. But you can be a stickler."

"For what?"

She held up a Post-it scratched with pencil marks.

"Ah." He understood. "For accountability."

"Something like that." She waved him off, giving the cake her full attention instead.

"Bye, Nadine." He grabbed the two boxes he had wrapped the night before, and headed back out to the pavilion.

Allison eyed the packages beneath his arm when he returned. "You have birthday wrapping paper?"

"I *bought* birthday wrapping paper," he corrected, holding out the two boxes to her.

She brought her hand to her chest, taking a step back on one foot. "No way. You get to do the honors for the girls. I thought any gifts should be given in person because of the other kids in attendance. I mean, everyone is getting a goodie bag, but I wanted any gifts for the girls to be privately given so they could savor the enjoyment of it. If that makes sense."

"It absolutely does," Shane said. "Well, then, let me find the girls because I've got something they can use for the upcoming scavenger hunt." He winked knowingly at Allison.

"Well, now, this I have to see." She followed him as he walked toward the girls, who were enjoying what was certainly not their first piece of cake. They sat side by side on a picnic table at the edge of the pavilion, their legs swinging beneath the bench seats.

Shane slid into the bench opposite the two of them, placing both matching boxes on the table next to each of their plates. Allison stood at his back, facing the girls. "Happy birthday, you two."

The twins immediately dropped their forks, reaching for the boxes. "Oooh!" Olivia gushed, a bit of chocolate icing smeared across her bottom lip.

"What is it?" Isla started shaking her box.

"Be careful. It might be breakable." Allison leaned forward, her shoulder brushing Shane's as she reacted on impulse to the girl's sudden move. His breath hitched, but she righted herself rather than linger, disappearing from his line of sight again.

"It's okay," he told Isla. "You can't break what's inside there. Go ahead," he urged them both. "Open it."

Shane saw the girls look to Allison as if for permission.

But then their fingers worked quickly to tear the paper, dive into the cardboard and fish out what was inside.

"Yay!" They rejoiced even before they fully admired the contents: a pink bandanna, an animal identification booklet, binoculars on a string and something in a velvet pouch.

"A star!" Isla held high the shiny badge that tumbled out of hers.

Shane pointed to his own sterling pin affixed to his shirt pocket. "You two are now official state park junior rangers."

"Oooh!" Olivia echoed.

"What's a junior ranger?" Isla didn't look up as she tried to work the badge's clasp. "Does it mean I'm a boss of something?"

Allison laughed. "That's kind of what it means, right, Shane?"

He hadn't thought about the best way to explain this, so he simply spoke the words that came to mind first. "It means that you are part of a very special group of people who get to wear a badge at this park. People who do that are in charge of making sure nature is cared for and that—"

"We care for Lucky," Isla cut in.

"Lucky isn't nature," Olivia corrected. "He's a dog."

"Have you met Lucky?" Isla cocked her head at Shane.

"Yes." It was just like kids to get sidetracked, so Shane wrapped up his speech. "You can wear the badge whenever you want. Be proud of it, and be good park rangers."

"Junior rangers," Isla reminded him.

"Of course." He smiled. "Junior rangers."

Isla got her clasp open, and Allison stepped around the table to pin the badges onto the girls. "Can we go on the scavenger hunt now?" She picked up her binoculars.

"Almost." Allison affixed Olivia's badge and told the girls, "Let's go get a drink of water, and then we'll get started."

"Yay!" the girls echoed together.

"And what do you say to Mr. Shane?" she prompted.

"Thank you!" In a flash, the girls ran around the table to where Shane sat, wrapping him in a half bear hug of appreciation—one girl on each side of him. He leaned down to hug the girls back. "My pleasure." Only when he heard a click did he look up from the huddle to see Allison snapping a photograph of them on her phone.

"I had to." She shrugged, a look of pure joy written all over her face.

And while Shane couldn't see what he looked like in that moment, he guessed he was looking pretty joyful himself.

Allison and several of the CASA volunteers rounded up the kids under age ten for the nature scavenger hunt while several of the preteens and teens in attendance, along with some of the more active adults, splintered off into groups for nature strolls organized by Ranger Lucas. The park's miles of color-coded trails were well marked, and a nearby mile-long trail was recommended by Shane. The oval loop started with a scenic, sweeping view of the valley along the limestone edge of the bluff on which part of the park grounds sat, followed by a winding gravel trail down into some of the wooded valley itself where Cottonwood Creek passed through. Other trails forked off from the one-mile loop, but this centralized trek was perfect for beginners.

"I've been on that trail dozens of times." Allison was assuring a hesitant fellow CASA volunteer, who had never explored the trail system. "You'll love it."

"I'm not much of a hiker," the woman admitted.

"Just stay on the path, and take it at your own pace. The harder trails are much farther below this one, so you'll be fine." She nodded toward Shane. "Plus, a ranger is never far away, so you have nothing to worry about."

"He looks trustworthy."

"He's in charge of the park for a reason." Allison passed the woman a water bottle and a reassuring look. "Follow his lead."

Shane held his hand high in the air, willing everyone to gather round as the nature stroll began. Allison, Nancy and several others stayed with the younger ones to start the scavenger hunt that was going to be kicked off by Ranger Garrett. A few adults remained under the pavilion, chatting and nibbling on leftover food at the tables. Everyone was finding their activity of choice.

"I can't get these bin-doc-ulars over my crown," a small voice called.

"It's bin-oc-ulars."

"I don't care," the voice called again. "It's bin-over me!"

Allison's past months of knock-knock joke banter with the twins had obviously resulted in them internalizing some puns, which made Allison smile to herself.

Allison walked toward the girls where Isla had tangled a web of string into her hair and through her plastic tiara. "Let me." She reached out to help.

Olivia paced around them both, proud as royalty at having gotten her binoculars into place around her neck without any trouble.

"There." Allison scooped up Isla's hair into a finger-combed ponytail before letting it cascade down her neck and settle over the string. "Now you're all ready for the scavenger hunt."

"I forgot my book!" Isla turned on a dime, racing away from Allison back to the pavilion to get the animal booklet that Shane had given them.

"I have mine." Olivia held up hers with a coy smile.

Isla came back, panting from her sprint. "Got it." She held it up like a gold medal. "I'm ready now."

"Okay, then. Nature trekkers, let's start our hunt!" She led the girls to the group of other children who also were participating, gathered under the shade of an oak tree. The slightly milder weather from earlier in the day was inching upward, with the summertime sun announcing itself a little more firmly. Allison wished she had grabbed her sunglasses, but they were back in a tote bag at the pavilion. Instead, she shielded her eyes with her hand as everyone listened to Ranger Garrett share some of the rules for the hunt, specifying what types of items the children would be searching for.

Garrett passed out small reusable tote bags to everyone. "Place any feathers you find, any leaves from the trail and your two rocks into this bag. Remember," he stressed, "only two, so look carefully for the ones you want to take back to the headquarters to identify."

"Can we pick flowers?" a girl asked.

"Thanks for reminding me." Garrett pointed toward the trail. "Wildflowers are protected on the trails, and we want to leave them to grow so everyone can enjoy them. No picking the flowers."

"Hear that?" Olivia leaned into Isla and echoed, "No picking the flowers."

"I'm a junior ranger." Isla pointed to the badge pinned to her pink T-shirt. "I follow the rules."

Those words were music to Allison's ears.

"Are we ready?" Garrett walked a few steps backward to lead the crowd, as he counted the number of participants.

"We're ready!" Fun replies of excitement followed his lead, and the scavenger hunt, just like the group on the nature stroll, was off.

* * *

Flora and fauna were alive throughout Cottonwood Creek State Park. The kids got to see butterflies in flight, lizards dashing across the gravel, grasshoppers springing like popcorn kernels from the tall grass and even a horned toad in the shade of one of the benches.

"I'm not sitting there," another little girl vowed, taking a wide turn around the spot.

"I want to see it!" called a different little boy, and Garrett crouched down next to the amphibious resident and explained a few facts about toads to those who gathered around to listen.

Allison had seen plenty of creatures great and small on her many runs through the park, but seeing them through the eyes of children was a precious sight. Even those who were reticent about some of the creepier, crawlier ones could appreciate others.

"I want to see a bird." Isla hurried next to the girl who was hoping for a winged visitor instead of the toady one, and she offered her binoculars to help.

The girls were interacting so well that Allison vowed to take them on individual trail hikes now that kindergarten was over for them. It might help give Mia and Michael a bit of a break, too, on weekends as summer stretched onward.

"I'm hot." Olivia stopped dead in her tracks, saying to no one in particular.

"There's a water fountain around the bend of that tree." Allison, the girls and the rest of the group were still on one of the wide walking paths, though the kids wove in and out of the grassy areas and rocky inclines to scavenge for their treasures.

"And I have to go to the bathroom," Isla announced, leaving her binoculars with her new bird-watching friend as she ran to Allison.

"I have to go, too," Olivia echoed, abandoning her focus on the water fountain.

"Okay." Allison thought fast. There were restrooms by the pavilion, and the group wasn't actually that far from them. A tug on the hem of her shirt interrupted her thoughts.

"How do you work these things?" The girl to whom Olivia had given her binoculars was looking through them backward, trying to balance a water bottle in her hand as she did. She couldn't have been more than five years old. "Can you help me?"

"Yes," Allison automatically responded, crouching down toward the budding ornithologist. "Olivia, Isla." She motioned for the twins to come closer as she tried to help all three. Allison didn't want to leave this young girl, and why not send the twins back on the buddy system to the restroom? It may even be faster for the two girls to dash there on their own, and then they could retrace their steps to join the group again. Allison explained that plan.

"Okay," they promised, running as fast as their little legs could carry them back toward the pavilion area. Allison shielded her eyes as she watched them while also splitting her time with her new charge, who already seemed to want to attach herself to Allison's side.

"Let's try looking over here." Allison led the girl toward Mia and Michael, who were surrounded by a group of children, including their own, pointing at something in the far distance past the bluff.

"I think I see something!" The girl righted the binoculars, as Allison squinted in the direction the others were pointing, though without her sunglasses, she was having a hard time focusing on whatever was being tracked.

"I really should have grabbed those," she mumbled to herself, glancing in the direction of the pavilion and also thinking about the twins. "Mia?" She tapped her shoulder to get her attention. "Could you make sure to keep an eye on this one?" She motioned toward the pint-size human shadowing her side. "I've got to get something back at the pavilion, and I'm going to check on the twins."

"Where are they?" she asked, a note of warning in her words.

"Nothing to worry about," Allison assured her. "They just had to go to the restroom."

"Those two…" Mia's voice trailed.

"Yes, they're definitely a force." There was a double intensity of everything with the twins: double the demands, double the urges, double the actions.

That meant there should have always been double the eyes on them. Allison admonished herself for letting her guard down. "It won't take me long to corral them back this way, as long as—"

"Yes, I'll keep an eye on this one." Mia seemed to read Allison's mind as she took the hand of the little girl. She leaned down to help adjust the binoculars in order to get a better view of some birds encircling an area in the distance.

Now Allison could go check on the twins. She glanced at her smartwatch, unsure of the exact time they had taken off in the first place. It hadn't been that long, right?

Without seeing them, she had a nagging sense of something heavy and uncertain, a weight pulling on her. She'd be fine once the twins were safely back with her. Wouldn't she?

Chapter Twelve

"Now, if you'll look closely at this plant—" Shane brushed aside some hanging strands of Spanish moss attached to woody vines "—you'll see a plant that looks tropical and a bit out of place." Shane reached for the leaves of the plant, showcasing them so everyone could get a better look.

"Is that a palm tree?" one of Shane's nature stroll guests asked.

"Yes, it's a special variety called a dwarf Palmetto."

"What's a palm tree doing in this part of Texas?"

"Good question. Any guesses?" He fielded a few answers that got close to the right one, which was that the plant was simply native. "It's more common in swampy areas, like east Texas. But there are pockets of them that grow in spots that are especially moist. We've got a few clumps of them as well as single ones like this dotted throughout the park. Most of its trunk is underground." He pointed beneath the bright foliage and answered a few more questions about native plants.

"Did you hear that?" A woman froze, turning her ear toward a sound that others seemed to hear.

Shane asked, "What's going on?"

"I think someone is screaming." Others nodded, agreeing.

Shane cocked his ear to the wind and listened again,

reaching for the radio at his hip. He hadn't heard a call, so he checked his cell phone, which Nadine was more apt to use.

Nothing.

But he did hear the shrill sound when the voice rang out again, this time loud and clear.

Someone was in distress.

And it sounded like a person's name was being called.

Shane turned up the volume on his radio, requesting an All-Points Bulletin. One of the other rangers replied to his APB: "A child went missing from the pavilion."

"Who are we looking for?" Shane never let worry seize him until absolutely necessary. People sometimes wandered off from their parties at the park: a slow walker might lag behind on a trail or a group might split up at a trailhead. Kids sometimes got too distracted playing games and would duck out of sight for a bit. Innocent stuff. The park was a big place, and there were lots of places that someone might be.

Although having a child go missing during such a busy event did raise Shane's pulse, especially with as many kids as were part of The Saturday Stroll.

"Six-year-old in a pink shirt," came the voice reply. There was some static on the radio followed by indistinct chatter before Ranger Garrett added, "Two six-year-olds, actually. Twins."

Shane's blood pressure jumped. There was only one set of twins that he knew of at the event.

Thoughts of the girls who not a half hour before were eating cake and opening gifts flashed in Shane's mind as he confirmed the reply, telling the airwaves that he would be heading up to the main area via a side trail that sometimes parkgoers mistook for an outlet. "I'll have that trail covered."

"Roger that."

"Okay, gang." Shane stood tall and addressed the group.

"We'll put the nature stroll on hold because we're looking for the two birthday girls. Both have brunette hair, pink shirts and athletic shorts." He tried to remember other distinguishing features that might catch someone's eye from a distance or through brush, but all he could see in his mind's eye were their teetering tiaras and too-big binoculars.

No one in the group objected, and they started buddying up and talking among themselves about which ways they would head.

"Anybody who finds them on the upper part of the park grounds," Shane instructed, "should bring them back to the pavilion. If you find them on the trails, whistle three times to signal. You can still escort them back to the pavilion, but we need to know immediately when they are found."

"What about the lake?" someone asked.

Surely, the girls wouldn't have wandered all the way down there.

Would they?

"As soon as we know exactly when they went missing, we can establish a perimeter. The lake is not part of that. For now." Shane fought the bile that sprung up in his throat at the worst of thoughts that he wasn't going to entertain.

He couldn't go there.

All he knew at the moment was that the girls were in trouble. And this park ranger was going to do everything in his power to help them.

"They were on the trail, they went to the restroom and they didn't come back." Allison's voice wavered as she spoke.

"What time did you last see them?"

"I don't know. Quarter to two?" Her voice trembled. "Maybe."

"Okay." Shane glanced at his wristwatch. "Let's just say they arrived at the restrooms at ten to two—"

"But I don't know." Panic rose with her words. "I didn't see them there."

"You never saw them enter the restroom?"

"I didn't because I wasn't there. They were supposed to—" She choked on a sob, trying to recover. "They were supposed to be right back." Tears that had welled in the corners of her eyes spilled. She swiped at them quickly, trying to avoid Shane seeing them.

"Look—" he placed his hand on her elbow "—take a deep breath, okay? We've got coverage on the trails, the walking path, eyes throughout the park grounds. We are going to find them," he vowed.

Allison nodded, standing up straighter and looking him in the eyes for the first time since their conversation began. From surrender or maybe terror at the prospect of what could have happened, she collapsed into his chest as he put his arms around her. "It's going to be okay," he whispered, holding her upright in spite of her determined stance.

"I should have been watching them." She spoke with soft pity.

"No should'ves or could'ves." He gave her a supportive squeeze before pulling back and holding her at arm's length with his hands at her shoulders. "We're focused on what's happening now."

Allison gave a curt nod. "What can I do?"

"You can walk." Having her sit still would yield no results, and it would only heighten her worry. "Along the walking path you and the girls had taken, I want you to retrace the perimeter. Even though we've got people on it, check the grassy areas alongside it, and go farther down than when they left. Maybe they circled around and wound up on the other side of the group."

"Walking," she repeated. "I can do that."

"Or run." Shane gestured to her athletic shoes. "I know how much you enjoy that," he added, trying to add a bit of levity to their heavy conversation.

"I can do that, too."

"Keep your phone on you." He tapped his in his shirt pocket. "You'll know as soon as I do when there's any news."

"Same."

"Take water with you."

Allison was already pivoting, focused on her new task. But she turned for a split second to say, "Thank you," her eyes still rimmed with red but with a look of determination.

They were going to find those twins. Because not only was that the sole positive outcome, but also because Shane wasn't sure he could stand to see the look on Allison's face if they didn't.

The twins needed to be okay. They had to be.

Allison admonished herself for being so careless. Her comfort and familiarity on the trails of Cottonwood Creek had caused her to lower her guard, which she never should have done when it came to the care of the twins. Why hadn't she kept a constant eye on them?

She was their advocate—their protector—and she had failed.

As she brushed aside tall grasses and scanned beyond the normal perimeter of where they had walked, she tried to think like a precocious child.

If I were them, where would I be?

Asking that question allowed her to push aside the worst

of thoughts and think logically. Hiding somewhere? Taking cover from the sun? Out of sight with their binoculars?

Maybe that was it. Could the girls have been crouching or keeping quiet somewhere?

They loved to play hide-and-seek in Mia and Michael's backyard with the other kids in the house, so maybe they had done that? There were countless places to take cover in the park, from behind trees to beside boulders to inside lower dips of the rocky cliff on the bluff's edge...and then there was the lake...

No.

Allison stopped herself.

She would not think of perilous places like the cliff or the lake. Those thoughts were too much for her. There had to be a safer place for them to be.

Allison's legs started doing the thinking, moving on autopilot when her thoughts were scattershot. She picked up the pace as she advanced farther from the original trail they had been on, and that was when the detour idea kicked in.

Bingo!

In the distance when someone exited from the restrooms, there was a trail in the valley below that could be seen but not readily accessed.

Or—while it could—it would involve a detour.

There wasn't a wide gravel path to it like on their walking trail, but enterprising little legs could carry someone up and over the hillside to join the narrow running trail below. And someone with little legs might very well have mistaken that path for the one they had been on.

It was possible.

Allison surged with adrenaline, her own legs bolting forward as her running shoes carried her on sheer determination alone. She knew the park grounds and where all the trails connected. She not only had intimate knowledge in practice, but she also had a steel-trap memory of the winding, intersecting color-coded spaghetti models on park maps that she had memorized from years of running.

Through some brush, around a bend and down a slope, she could join the trail that would have otherwise taken her a much longer time to access. It was worth a shot because she didn't see any other heads bobbing along the slim portion of the path that was visible from above.

"Ouch!" She stopped jogging just long enough to reach toward a sharp pain near her foot. A thin scratch extended the width of her ankle, the work of some nasty, gnarly vine.

But at least it wasn't a snake.

As soon as she had that thought, though, adrenaline pumped harder. Yes, it was still early in summertime. Snakes were active, and their camouflage among the forest debris in the more wooded areas like she was heading made them all the more difficult to spot.

Would the girls know what to avoid? Or how to handle one if it crossed their path?

Or, worse, had they perhaps succumbed to an injury? If not a snake, then some other injury was possible…

Allison used her opposite leg to spring forward away from more of the vine's grasp, propelling herself back into a runner's rhythm. She'd worry about the cut later.

Shane had told her to walk, but she was going to run. Nothing would keep her from finding those girls.

"Olivia!" Allison took a deep breath. "Isla!" She heard echoes of the same calls from others who were joining in the search.

The only reply, however, were the crunch of leaves and the grind of gravel beneath her running shoes.

One foot. And then the other.

That was the way forward.

"Isla!" she called again. "Olivia!" Alternating their names gave her a new pattern on which to focus. She also tried to keep her breathing steady as her running shoes gripped the trail in rhythm.

This act that was usually meditative on the trail now felt labored and intense. Her voice kept calling, her eyes kept scanning and her heart kept hoping.

The trail would soon link to one that connected to the switchbacks. That seemed like such a far way for the girls to travel. Allison flicked her wrist to activate her smartwatch, slowing just enough to check the time. That was when her ears registered something.

Three whistles.

A loud, unmistakable sequence.

Allison's running ground to a halt, her body breathless and spent.

Someone had found them! Relief so strong hit her in a wave, and all her pent-up emotions poured out of her in tears.

She pressed the heels of her palms to her eyes to stop them before she started running again, toward the pavilion and toward the girls.

Chapter Thirteen

A group of adults was gathered in a huddle. Allison's legs couldn't take her there fast enough.

She had run back along the trails as soon as she heard the whistling and arrived at the makeshift command central beneath the pavilion. She recognized most everyone even with their backs turned to her, including Mia, Michael, Nancy, her mother, other CASA volunteers—and Shane.

"Have you found them?" Allison called as she sprinted toward the concrete edge of the pavilion, bounding onto it and joining the group. Her heart was racing a mile a minute. "The girls?" Her exhausted lungs choked out the desperate question.

Shane spun around, opening the huddle just enough for Allison to see something familiar come into view.

A shiny plastic tiara.

Atop the head of a smiling Isla.

Next to her was Olivia, her hair hanging loosely in her face, but unmistakably her just the same.

Allison brought her hand to her chest, soaking up gratitude at the scene as she gulped desperate breaths.

The sight of two sweaty six-year-olds never looked so sweet.

"Safe and sound." Shane extended his arm toward Allison,

bringing her into the group. She raced past him to get to the twins. Crouching low to where they were seated crisscross on the concrete, she cried, "Oh, girls!" She was ready to embrace them in a double hug and never let them go.

"You're sweaty." Olivia recoiled. The comment sucker punched Allison, not for its unexpectedness but for its ordinary nature.

"Oh, girls," she said again, this time more softly and gently.

"They had a little adventure," Nancy announced by way of explanation.

"Isla did it," Olivia tattled.

"You told me to," she fired back.

Allison reached to Olivia's hair, brushing it back with her fingers and admiring the face of the little girl who just moments ago she thought she might never see again. She reached toward Isla, placing her hand on her shoulder. "Where were you two?"

"Squirrel watching."

"Squirrel *chasing*," Olivia corrected her sister.

Isla held up her animal booklet. "We found one." She flipped the pages before stopping on one. "See?" She raised it higher for Allison's inspection and pointed at a picture.

"It was probably a fox squirrel," Shane offered. "Maybe a Mexican ground squirrel."

"Which one is gray?" Isla asked.

"Check the book," Olivia reprimanded.

"You can't read it, either." She turned away from her sister. "Which one?" She looked up at Shane.

"It was probably a Mexican ground squirrel," he answered, as if this was the most normal conversation in the world.

"See?" She whipped her head back around to Olivia, who crossed her arms over her chest and huffed.

Allison would get the full story later. The girls each had water bottles beside them, and aside from the sweat, they didn't appear to be harmed in the least.

Thankful, Allison could start to breathe normally for the first time since the search had begun.

Still, it was going to take her more than this moment to fully catch her breath. She stood up, her legs a bit shaky as Nancy grabbed her by the elbow. Her mother was at her side in a flash as well.

"Whoa," she said, steadying her. "Careful there."

Allison leaned on her mother's forearm. "Thanks, Mom." She stepped back once she felt her legs under her. "I think I need some water." Her own water bottle had dropped somewhere along the way, probably at the base of the trail. She had no memory of losing it, but she didn't remember much beyond her feet pounding the gravel after she heard those whistles.

"Let me get you something." Nancy spun away from her as her mother continued to steady her. But then she felt a different person's touch. Shane's masculine hand cupped her lower back, protectively keeping her upright.

"You okay?" He didn't remove his hand.

"I'm getting there." She took another step as Shane's hand fell. "I think I need to find the breeze again and cool down." Her mother agreed as she stepped away. Allison and Shane started walking toward where there was a cross breeze. "What happened?"

Shane guided her out of earshot of the girls at the edge of the pavilion. "It seems they had a nature adventure of their own."

"They were supposed to go to the restroom and come right back."

"Kids." He shrugged.

Allison had so many questions, but she started with one. "Where were they?"

"As I understand it," he began, voice steady, "they spotted a squirrel and wanted to follow it."

That sounded innocent enough, but the answer was not satisfying to Allison. "Where did they go?"

"It's hard to know, but they did end up at some point on the lower valley trail. The one visible from the hillside off the restrooms."

Allison knew that trail from the park maps, labeled like a green spaghetti thread. "I was on that trail."

Shane shrugged.

Her instincts had been right, but her timing had been wrong. "How did I miss them?"

"They also ended up in the maintenance shed."

"Wait." Allison's mind took a sharp left turn. "The one on the other side of the trail?"

"Ranger Lucas found them," Shane said.

"Were they—" Allison could barely speak, her questions forming faster than her voice could speak them.

Shane stopped her from assuming the worst. "They had gone in there after the squirrel. Although, if you ask Isla, that point is debatable. She says the squirrel didn't run in there."

"But they did?"

"Both of them," he confirmed.

"So when I was on the lower trail or others were passing close by the shed…" Allison was starting to understand the full sequence of events.

"They probably never even heard people calling their names." Shane shrugged again. "Or, if they did, they didn't want to answer and disturb the squirrel."

Allison's fears were assuaged, but it was still going to take some time for her to fully collect herself. Nancy appeared at her side. "Drink this."

Allison took the ice-cold water bottle, twisting the top and taking deep, refreshing gulps. She inhaled sharply as she brought the bottle to her side, thanking Nancy.

"We don't need you getting dehydrated today. One crisis at a time is enough."

And even if Nancy's words were meant to be playful, the choice of them still struck Allison.

Crisis.

Yes, it had been exactly that. Two girls had gone missing. Two girls whom Allison was supposed to be watching.

All her life, she was fluent in the language of failure: broken relationships, setbacks at school, hiccups at work. But today's turn of events had taken things to a whole other level.

Falling short in her own life was one thing. But falling short when others were counting on her was a whole other thing.

Maybe she wasn't as responsible as she had thought.

Maybe she wasn't the best advocate for Olivia and Isla.

Because as her mind continued with snatches of scenarios that wouldn't stop, it was easy to see how things could have ended terribly. Her failure with the twins was one of tremendous proportion. Gutted, the failure of the afternoon felt as wide as the grounds of Cottonwood Creek State Park.

And even someone as responsible as Shane Hutton—or anyone else at Cottonwood Creek, for that matter—couldn't convince her otherwise.

"Guess you didn't expect that kerfuffle with the twins during The Saturday Stroll." Nadine greeted Shane as he walked through the headquarters of the office. "Never a dull moment."

"I'll say." Shane closed the door behind him, leaning

against it for a reprieve as he enjoyed the relative silence and the indoor air-conditioning. His park ranger uniform was not as comfortable as T-shirts and shorts that most everyone at The Saturday Stroll had worn.

"Do you want to start the paperwork now, or—"

"I'll get to it."

"It's best while the details are fresh." Nadine was forever working toward a gold medal in the Olympic sport of nagging. "I'm just saying."

Shane took his responsibility to write an incident report for events at the park that involved any form of search and rescue—even when no outside agencies were involved—seriously. It helped with accountability.

"Because you tend to forget the details."

"I said I'll get to it, Nadine." Shane was going to have to force his fingers on the keyboard to complete the report that would stay filed in a digital folder on his office computer, even if no one questioned anything. But on the chance that someone did—or, worse, that someone challenged the park system at a later date over the incident—he would be covered.

"Just reminding you." Nadine was doing more than that. "And, while you're at it, are you going to put your application in for permanent ranger here? You can do that as well while you're in there."

His digital signature had barely dried on the west Texas position application, which Nadine didn't know about. "You know I'm only an interim park ranger here."

"That's why you need to get that application in."

Shane wasn't going to do that, but he wasn't going to entertain that conversation with Nadine. He stepped away from the door. He felt himself powering down like a waning cell phone battery, definitely needing a charge.

"Let me know when you want me to proof the other paperwork."

He didn't need to be that quick with protocol.

In fact, he suddenly didn't want to be in his office at all. "Actually, I'm going down to the lake."

"But I'm closing the entrance in five minutes."

"Good." Shane didn't want any more distractions. He needed to clear his head before he buried himself in his computer.

"And I'm leaving after that."

"Also good." Shane put his hand on the door. "You should. It will be closing time."

"And you?"

Shane lowered his sunglasses back over his eyes. "Have a good evening, Nadine."

He opened the door and fixed his sights on the lake. A brisk walk around the perimeter would be enough to clear his mind and might even be enough to push aside those images of the afternoon's search for Olivia and Isla that he was having a hard time shaking.

He didn't expect anyone to be at the lake so close to the park's closing time. Most patrons readily obeyed the hours and heeded the signage about headquarter closure and vacating the premises, especially since so many of the people who came through the gates were locals. But every once in a while, he would have to round up stragglers and direct them toward the exit.

Looks like he might have to do just that with one such straggler today.

A woman sat alone at a picnic table, a large tote bag obscuring her profile from a distance. A ball cap shielded her face as she looked down, seemingly at something in her lap.

"Closing time soon, ma'am," Shane called when he was within earshot.

The ball cap rose to reveal topaz-colored eyes that he recognized.

"Allison." He picked up his pace to close the gap between them. "I thought you left after the cleanup was finished at the pavilion."

"I couldn't." She lowered her head again.

"Are you okay?"

"I hardly know." She lifted her chin somewhat but seemed to look past Shane's gaze.

He took a seat opposite her, sliding onto the wooden bench and lifting his sunglasses atop his head. "Talk to me."

"If I do," she said, "I'll start to cry."

"That's okay." Shane had dealt with a lifetime of tears, the result of a variety of situations. Some familial. Some professional. And even some personal. "Try me."

"This day..." Allison started, her head tilting back as if to soak up strength from the disappearing sun.

"I've had worse," Shane offered, trying to help her keep perspective.

In the absence of a response from her, he continued.

"And you almost did. The first time I met you? On the trails?" he prompted. "You were almost bitten by a snake that day."

"I wasn't almost bitten." She leveled her gaze and looked at him for the first time in a meaningful way across the table. "That copperhead was harmless. And you know it."

"Maybe." Shane knew full well that it was, though he wanted her to think coolly. "But anything could have happened."

"Yes, anything could have happened," she said in a finite tone. "Today."

"But it didn't. Not today." There were worst-case possibilities, but none had come to fruition regarding the girls. "The twins were found safe. It was nobody's fault that they went missing."

"It was mine. I know that kids can't be watched every minute of the day. I wasn't trying to do that." Allison's threat of crying abated as she found words to express herself. "But I shouldn't have assumed they were responsible enough to be left alone. That was a mistake on my part, and it could have ended in—"

"But it didn't," Shane cut in. "That's the thing, Allison. You didn't do anything wrong."

"Then why does it feel like I did?"

Shane chewed on that question, settling on a one-word answer. "Guilt."

Allison seemed to contemplate that answer with equal consideration. They let silence settle between them, but it wasn't an uncomfortable feeling. On the contrary, it seemed both necessary and reassuring.

Allison wasn't crying.

Shane wasn't worried.

So maybe this conversation was working for them both.

The sun stretched its rays beyond the horizon line, creating a deep chasm of shimmering semicircles. Colors danced together in a late-afternoon symphony of the sky. "That sight never gets old." Shane looked over Allison's shoulder, which prompted her to turn toward the sun. She stayed turned away from him for a while, perhaps absorbing the pretty scene. Or maybe she was still thinking about his answer of guilt, sitting with that word as well.

Sometimes, with women, it was hard to tell.

But Allison wasn't running away. She wasn't squirming in her seat. She was staying.

With him.

That had to count for something.

"You know," he tried a different approach, "when I was about five, I tried to run away from home."

Allison turned back around. "Why did you want to run away?"

Shane mentally scrolled through the answers he could have said. "A little bit of everything, I guess."

"At age five?"

"It was a tough age. Or," Shane recalled, "at least it felt that way at the time."

"Why?"

Shane placed his sunglasses on the table, twisting the earpiece as if the rim was a spinning top. "My family decided to take in a foster child."

"Oh." Allison sat up taller. "Did that child become your sibling?"

"I thought he might. His name was David. He was just a baby." Shane's memories of some parts of his childhood were a bit fuzzy, but details like this were crystal clear. "He only stayed a couple of months, but my parents doted on him, and I thought I was being replaced."

"Even though you wanted him to be your brother?"

"I didn't know what I wanted." Shane tried to find more language to express his conflicting feelings from that time long ago. But as sometimes happened when he confronted his past, certain memories crowded out all else.

Not all of them were happy ones.

Allison leaned forward. "Where did you go?"

"Just took a walk outside. Walks—" he stilled the sunglasses "—have always seemed to help me."

"Must have been some walk."

"I didn't come back until after dark."

"Your parents must have been so worried."

Shane let more silence take hold, as he thought again about his earlier answer of guilt. Did he always harbor that? How could he, if he was born to parents who seemed to have a very different relationship with that emotion? Whereas he harbored feelings of guilt more times than he could count in his lifetime, they never did, even when they did things wrong.

To Allison's credit, she didn't press the conversation or rush to accelerate Shane's trip down memory lane. She simply held the silence with him.

"Did you ever run away again?"

"No." That was the truth. "But I thought about it." That was also the truth.

"That seems normal. Kids have lots of conflicting emotions, and childhood can be a lot to deal with."

"Yes." Shane had made it through his, but not without scars. Foster kids came and went, and the more he witnessed patterns and saw his parents' distraction from him, the deeper the cuts became.

"You know…" Allison reached her hands to the bench seat, grabbing the wood and swaying ever so slightly as she spoke. "I've always tried to lean in to my emotions. Failure, success, whatever. Maybe it's not always the healthiest approach—or maybe it is?" She stopped moving just long enough to say, "I think I just need to sit with my feelings about today a little longer. Does that make sense?"

"It does."

"I'm not telling you to go." Her hand moved toward Shane but stopped short. "Not at all."

He was listening to her. And he heard her. "You just want to sit."

"Yes." She brought her hand back down to the bench. "And will you sit with me? For a bit longer?"

"Yes," he answered, thinking there was nowhere on earth he'd rather be.

Chapter Fourteen

"I'm glad you came today." Allison's mother pulled her in for a hug on the steps of Cottonwood Creek Community Church.

"I thought twice about it," Allison admitted.

"Oh, honey." Her mother tilted her head. "Are you still thinking about yesterday? Because yesterday was so wonderful."

"And scary." Allison pulled back, keeping her emotions in check as best she could.

During the service, that had been a difficult thing, especially when the choir sang a hymn that reminded Allison of the high cost of love and letting her guard down. She worked hard to keep herself composed in the pew as worst-case scenarios regarding the twins ran through her mind.

But afterward, the weight of it all threatened with tears that might spill at any moment.

"I've seen you with Olivia and Isla before. But..." Her mother held Allison at arm's length, not letting her go in spite of the distance she tried to force. "I have never seen them so full of joy and genuine happiness as I did yesterday. You, my dear, did that."

"But they went missing." Allison voice was barely above a whisper.

"And they came back." She gave her daughter a squeeze before dropping her hands. "Honey, don't be so hard on yourself."

"That's easy for you to say."

"Allison," her mother began again, "between you and Jessica, I know all about being hard on yourself. Trust me."

Her mother's tone caught her attention. "What do you mean? Were we bad kids?"

Her mother's demeanor softened. "You were wonderful children." She reached a hand to Allison's hair, tucking a loose strand behind her ear. "And you have grown up to be equally wonderful women. You and Jessica both."

Allison released a heavy sigh. "I don't feel so wonderful right now."

Allison's mother took a step back and said, "Then you need to get over that."

Allison chewed on those firm words as she thought about how she was supposed to simply let an experience like almost losing two children in a large state park not affect her. "How do you move forward when it comes to the really hard stuff?"

"Caring for children involves ups and downs. There are plenty of good moments and plenty of scary moments." Her hands came together in a steeple position. "If I could have prevented all the scary moments, I would have. But no one has that power."

"But people have responsibility."

"True." Her mother unclasped her hands. "And with that responsibility, we love others, we look out for them as best we can and we move forward. No matter," she underscored, "what hurt we are facing or what regret we might feel."

"I do have regret." Allison blew out another breath.

"For becoming a CASA volunteer?"

"What? No," Allison emphasized. "Absolutely not. I've loved every moment of volunteering."

Her mother raised an eyebrow. "Every moment?" She repeated the words for Allison to hear.

"Yes." As Allison listened to her instinctive reply, the truth of what she was saying settled into her. She did love every moment with Olivia and Isla, and being a part of their lives.

The ups.

The downs.

It was all part of the bargain.

"Are you going to stop being a CASA volunteer?"

Allison shook her head.

"Good. Because I don't think you should. You're good for them."

And they're good for me, too. Caring for them had been a balm for Allison the past few months, soothing over the emptiness that had been left in the wake of her last relationship. The twins had healed her own heart in ways they may never know and that even Allison was having a hard time understanding.

"When we share our burdens, we lighten the load." Her mother's counsel echoed the words of the pastor during the service.

Tears that just moments earlier had felt so certain to come had dissipated. The tension in her body that she had held since midday on Saturday was now being replaced by a lightness that Allison was ready to embrace.

"Thank you, Mom." Allison spoke the words quietly as she stepped forward for a final hug, which her mother was swift to offer.

"I love you, Allison."

"I love you, too."

As her mother's arms wrapped around her, their conversation echoed in Allison's mind.

It dawned on her that while her mother had complimented Allison's role with the twins, she said nothing about actual motherhood.

Did her very own parent not see her as mother material?

And if that was true, was it any wonder that Allison didn't see that in her future as well?

"Why don't you come by this afternoon for a visit? We can relax with some tea on the front porch." They did usually spend some quality time together on Sundays, after church.

Her mother did always know the right thing to say. "Sure." Allison added, "I'll stop by after checking in with Mia and seeing how the girls are doing."

"You should definitely do that. See you soon." Her mother waved goodbye, and Allison made her way to her car.

As she ate some leftovers for lunch at home, she texted Mia. They exchanged rapid messages, including some photos of the girls playing with a new set of kickballs they had gotten on Saturday. The images were framed by the Westmorelands' backyard.

"Fences are safe," Allison mumbled to herself, still fighting the feelings that she had spoken about with her mother. But she was glad for the twins and could at least rest easier in knowing that their love of the outdoors hadn't been permanently altered by what happened on Saturday. It made going to her mother's for the afternoon a bit more comfortable.

After a full day, Allison had to agree with her mother. Sharing the burden did lighten the load.

When she returned to work on Monday, she was greeted by beginning-of-the-week billing responsibilities that monopolized most of her time.

Problem solving made the work day pass quickly, and in the hour between the last patients arriving and the closure of the clinic for the day, Dr. Zambrano stepped in front of Allison's desk. "Knock, knock."

Allison looked up. "Dr. Zambrano, hi."

"Just coming to see if the gift bags all got distributed on Saturday."

Of course Dr. Zambrano would want to know. "Oh yes, everyone was so thankful. In fact—" Allison reached for her cell phone inside her purse "—I have a few pictures of the kids and the CASA volunteers. May I show you?"

"I'd be delighted. I need some good news today." Dr. Zambrano wheeled an available chair from a nearby cubicle and sat next to Allison as she scrolled through some of the photographs she had taken near the beginning of the event, prior to the twins going missing. Everything on her camera roll looked sparkly and perfect. Allison added context as well as names for some of the people in the photos.

"Are those your CASA twins?" A close-up of the girls with their toothy grins and tiaras as they enjoyed their birthday cake slices looked like something out of a bakery advertisement. "They're adorable."

"They are." Allison couldn't argue with that.

"How often do you see them?"

"Multiple times a week." She was supposed to visit them again on Thursday after work but was still hesitating in light of what happened Saturday. "They're six years old now, so..." Maybe one missed evening wouldn't be noticed from the girls, who still weren't skilled at understanding calendars and days of the week. That might give Allison the will to face them again at a later time because she didn't know if she had the strength to do so with the weight of regret still rearing its ugly head, even though she thought she had dealt with it.

"I'm glad the clinic could support that CASA event and those girls. Let me know if you need anything else." Dr. Zambrano rose, pushing her chair back into place and thanking Allison again for showing her the photographs. "Love seeing smiles."

Allison certainly did, too.

As she looked at the girls' grins again, she tamped down the regret that she was unfairly holding on to. She did want to see them. She did want to continue to advocate for them. Because even if she didn't do everything quite right all the time, those girls didn't know the difference. In their world, Allison was love.

If she could be that to two precious souls, what else did she really need in her life?

Allison had just finished a five-mile loop in the park on Wednesday when Shane caught her outside the headquarters. "I think you should bring the twins back to the park," he said.

"Excuse me?" Allison popped out her earbuds, making sure she heard him correctly.

"I said, I think the twins should come back to the park, with you."

Allison's seesawing feelings of the past few days made her admit, "I'm not sure."

"They enjoyed the pedal boats. They had so much fun running around at The Saturday Stroll."

"And they went missing there, too," she reminded him.

"Have you talked to them about it?"

"No."

"Then how do you know they have those memories?"

Allison slipped her earbuds into her pocket. This was turning into more of a conversation than she expected. "I imagine that they might not need to be reminded of that anytime soon."

"Memories are a funny thing." Shane rested a hand on his utility belt. "It's hard to know what kids remember and what they choose to forget."

"The good stuff." Allison added, "Only. That's all I want them to remember from Saturday."

"They probably do."

Allison hoped that was true.

"But the park can always be a place of new memories. Good ones. Fun ones." Shane urged, "You know that."

Allison did. Her time on the trails was valuable, and her runs were priceless for both her physical health as well as her mental health. "Though it doesn't seem right to put the girls on the trails."

"Who said anything about trails?"

"Then what do you mean?"

Shane shifted his stance. "You know there's so much more to do here than trails. In fact…" The tone of his voice changed to one that Allison didn't quite understand. "I've been thinking about The Saturday Stroll and wanted to get your feedback."

Allison took a deep breath, then said, "It was a good idea, but parts of it could have been executed better."

"I disagree."

She was surprised. "You're entitled to your opinion."

Shane squared his shoulders and told Allison, "I think it needs to be repeated. What do you think about turning The Saturday Stroll into a monthly event?"

Allison wrung her hands together, absently twisting her fingers in disbelief at what she was hearing. "You want to do all of this again?"

"Why not?" Shane's words held no hesitation. "It doesn't

have to look exactly the same as the first one. We can change it up."

"We?" Allison's idea was for a onetime event. She wanted the girls to have a birthday celebration, not for her to be roped into something on a revolving basis.

"You were so good organizing everything that I just thought—"

"Let me stop you right there." Allison held up her hand. "I know my limits, and I can't commit to something monthly. Not when I've already got so much on my plate."

"Fair enough," Shane said. "Then how about a compromise?"

"What did you have in mind?"

Shane thought about it. "Four times a year. Summer, fall, winter and spring."

A Saturday Stroll once every three months at the park sounded manageable. "For CASA?"

"Absolutely. But with less decorations and food." Shane had obviously already thought through some specifics. "Instead, it could be more of a picnic-style atmosphere. Everyone could bring a dish, the volunteers and kids could have a potluck and then everyone could just hang out. Nature walks and scavenger hunts, totally optional," he promised.

A picnic in a public park with an open invitation did sound like an easy thing to organize.

"Would Nancy go for that?" Shane asked. "And what about all the kids? They really did have fun just being outdoors."

Allison took a deep breath of the fresh air that surrounded her. She couldn't argue with that.

"I guess we've already done the hard part." Allison found herself using the same inclusive *we* that Shane had used.

"Exactly." Shane made it all sound so easy. "Garrett and Lucas also now know the ropes. So they can help even if…"

Allison knew the words he wasn't saying. "Even if you're not here?"

Shane's voice grew quieter. "I don't know where I'm going to end up working. But I do know that right now, I'm here in Cottonwood Creek, and I really think this is a special event that needs to continue."

Allison couldn't argue with that.

"So what do you say?" The tone of his voice lifted. "Saturday Stroll at the park again in September?"

That was a long enough time away, and who knows how the twins would truly feel about coming back by then? It did seem a shame to keep them from such a beautiful place, even if one experience was soured. Allison nodded. "Okay."

"You're the best." Shane gave a low whistle of satisfaction.

At least Allison could predictably make one person happy.

Since Shane's Zoom interview was happening on Friday afternoon with park personnel for the Big Bend Ranch State Park position, he used Thursday to get a few things in order. "Nadine, can you run a report on park pass numbers?"

"What do you want to know?"

"Totals." But to measure the impact of The Saturday Stroll, he needed to drill down. "Also, I need to know how many season passes were issued so far this month." Measurable impact might be slim, but he could use percentages and make the data favorable for his purposes of showing the initiative's impact.

"Printed or emailed?" Nadine practically yawned the words. Granted, spreadsheets were not the most exciting morning task.

"Email is fine. Thank you, Nadine."

"You know," Nadine went on, "I can tell you what I've been seeing just by who's been coming through here."

"I bet you can." Her eagle eyes caught everything from her perch at the park's entrance. "But I need something concrete."

"As if my word isn't good enough."

Even when he tried not to, Shane still seemed to be sucked into Nadine's vortex of negativity. Although it wasn't just Shane. Nadine did that with everyone. "So have you been seeing an increase?"

"Some." She named a few of the community members who had bought park passes.

"That's fantastic."

"Then, we still have our regulars." She added with a sly tone, "Like Allison."

Shane wasn't sure where she was going with this.

"I saw you talking to her yesterday."

"I talk to a lot of people."

"About continuing The Stroll?"

"Yes, as a matter of fact."

"Good." Nadine smacked her lips. "So I guess you must have already put in your application to make Cottonwood Creek your permanent home—"

"No." Shane shut down her speculating. "I haven't, as a matter of fact."

"Oh. I see." Her lips pursed as she struck a defiant pose.

Shane wasn't going to lie to Nadine. "I know that the board is going to be calling in applicants soon, and I'm just a holdover to that."

"You don't have to be."

"I knew that coming into this job," Shane added, "and you did, too. It's an interim position for a reason."

"The state of Texas plays fast and loose with its words sometimes." She waved a dismissive hand.

"Not when it comes to employment titles." The park system was a well-oiled machine in some respects.

"Titles are…" Nadine tugged at her earlobe before working her fingers against her earring, still looking at Shane. "Silly sometimes."

"Coming from the woman who's a stickler for rules."

Nadine gave a shake of her head. "Back to The Saturday Stroll. You told me you wanted to repeat it. Did Allison agree?"

"She did, in fact." He easily recalled their conversation from the day before. "The event will continue for people who need it."

"It just won't continue with *you*." The silence that followed that biting comment was enough to hear a tree fall in a lonely forest.

"The Saturday Stroll is important," Shane stressed.

"Important?" Nadine arched an eyebrow, thin from years of overplucking. "But not important enough for you to see it through?"

"That's not fair."

"Isn't it?" Her side-eye drilled into him.

"I don't have a monopoly on this project."

"It was your idea."

And, thanks to Allison, it was able to happen. "No man is an island."

"Pfft!" Nadine practically spit. Good thing there had been nothing but words in her mouth. "What kind of babbling is that?"

Shane thought of a better way to explain. "It means that it takes a lot of people to make things happen. And this Saturday Stroll now belongs to Cottonwood Creek. Not just to me."

"So you're just leaving it here?"

"Yes."

"When you leave?"

"Yes."

"I see."

Nadine's face fell in a look of disappointment. Shane knew that expression. So many times in his life, he had seen that same look wash over people close to him. His whole life had been an exercise in disappointing others.

Still, he couldn't disappoint himself.

"I'll get you that data." Nadine spun around to face her computer, putting an end to their conversation.

"Thank you, Nadine." Shane walked back to his office.

He needed a job as big as his dreams. West Texas had always called to him, and with the opportunity open, he wasn't going to let that dream simply pass him by. He was going to chase it.

With his interview just a day away, he needed to be armed with talking points and verifiable data to bolster his credentials. The Saturday Stroll to benefit CASA had been a success, and he would leverage everything he could from it to show that to others.

Then, when he was long gone from Cottonwood Creek, he could still rest easy in the knowledge that he was leaving the people behind with something meaningful. He had every faith that Allison could continue it, especially with Nadine and the rest of the park staff to assist. His head told him not to worry.

But his heart told him that leaving the people he cared about behind might be more challenging than he anticipated.

Chapter Fifteen

Allison called Mia on Friday during her lunch break, a half-eaten peanut butter sandwich in one hand, her cell phone in the other.

Mia answered on the fourth ring. "Hey, Allison, sorry." She sounded out of breath. "I almost couldn't get to the phone."

"Are you okay?"

"Yes." Her lips smacked on the other end. "But I have cookie batter all over my fingers."

"Sounds delicious." Allison stared at her bland sandwich.

"I sure hope they turn out that way. It's an activity with the kids."

"All of them?"

"Yeah," she confirmed, "all five kids in the kitchen."

Mia and Michael's own three biological children were also out of school for the summer, along with the twins. "That's a lot of cookies."

"You're telling me." The phone muffled as Mia instructed something to one of the kids that Allison couldn't quite hear.

"Is now a bad time?"

"No." Mia's voice sounded clearer as she insisted, "It's a busy time, but never a bad time to hear from you. What's going on?"

Allison had a chance to reflect on what Shane said regarding the twins, and she wanted to approach that plan with Mia. "I wanted to ask about weekend time with the girls—"

"They are all yours." Mia was swift with the offer and quick to explain. "This is my first summer with five and it's...intense."

"I can imagine." Though in the background, Allison was hearing all kinds of wonderful sounds of laughter, joy and family life. That was in absolute contrast to her own home environment, which was quiet. When she did have occasion to bake chocolate chip cookies, she did so alone in her household of one.

The warmth of Mia's home sounded absolutely wonderful.

"I was thinking," Allison started again, "that maybe a trip back to Cottonwood Creek Park would be good for the girls. But I wanted to run that by you. Have they been talking about The Saturday Stroll?"

"Nonstop."

"Really?" Maybe the memories were too fresh, and this was too soon for them.

"They walk around with those binoculars every time they go outside. They keep calling themselves junior rangers. And they're asking me all kinds of reptile questions that I don't have the answers for."

"So they don't seem to be traumatized from getting lost?"

"Traumatized?" Mia chuckled. "Not in the least. Allison, those girls had the time of their lives thanks to you. The park, the birthday party. They were princesses for the day. It's all I can do not to take them back to the park myself just to get them to—"

"Ohh, are we going to the park?" Allison heard one of the girls call out in the background.

A lightness filled Allison. She had worried that the park

experience of The Stroll had been tainted for them, but Mia confirmed it was exactly the opposite.

"Um," Mia whispered. "What should I tell them?"

The girls were ready. Cottonwood Creek was calling to them, as it always seemed to do to Allison herself.

Shane had been right.

Allison's broad smile was hidden only by the fact that this was an audio call. "Tell them I'll pick them up after work today. Five thirty sharp." She bounced her heels against the floor beneath her desk, already looking forward to it. "Tell them to bring their binoculars."

Allison finished her afternoon projects at the clinic, then drove straight to the Westmorelands. Mia greeted her at the front door, holding out a plastic zipper bag with chocolate chip cookies. "We survived."

"These look delicious." Allison grabbed the bag, her sweet tooth on high alert. "Cookie baking is always a good idea."

"They're not much to look at. But the kids had fun making them today."

"These will be a perfect snack at the park. Thank you." Allison stepped inside the house, careful not to trip over Lucky, who ran in circles underfoot. She made her way to the kitchen where all the children were gathered around the center island of the large, open-concept area. "Taylor, Trevor, Tara, did you help bake these cookies, too?" She held up the bag.

"We all did." Taylor, as the oldest, answered with conviction.

"I measured the flour," Trevor said. "Tara added the chocolate."

"That was the fun part." Tara's eyes lit with the brightness of a Christmas morning surprise.

"I bet." Allison loved the teamwork approach that the kids were articulating.

"What about us? Tell the part that we did, Taylor," Olivia insisted.

"Olivia and Isla got to put them in the bags."

"Once they were cool," Isla corrected.

"It sounds like quite an assembly line." Allison looked to Mia, who had organized it all.

"I'll say." Mia placed two mixing spoons into a bowl at the edge of the sink. "And since the kitchen is still a bit of a disaster, it may turn into a pizza night tonight."

"Pizza!" The kids sang a chorus of support for that idea.

"Are you sure this excursion to the park won't push dinner too late for you?"

Mia dismissed the concern with a wave. "Please. We ate dessert first. Pizza can be delivered later."

"You're an amazing woman." Allison admired her friend.

"Amazing women," Mia reminded Allison, "keep good company."

"I'll remember that."

"You should." Mia turned her attention back to the twins. "Okay, you two." She clapped her hands in the air, walking in micro-steps behind the twins as she guided them to the front door like a mother hen. "Let's get your shoes on."

"But what about Lucky?" Olivia frowned.

"Lucky's going to stay here," Allison answered. She always had Mia's back in more ways than one.

"You mean he can't go to the park with us?" Isla pouted.

"I don't think Allison has room in her car."

"Yes, she does!" Olivia pleaded. "Please?"

"Sorry, honey. Not today." Allison bent down as she answered Olivia, helping her with one shoe in the process. "He'll be much happier staying at home anyway."

"But he might like the pedal boats."

"Or the trails."

"He liked being at The Saturday Stroll."

The girls' pleading was relentless.

"Yes," Allison conceded. "And he can come to the next one." She and Shane had yet to firm up a date, but sometime in September would be another good outing for Lucky. Today she was taking Shane's advice and had decided to bring the girls back to the park for—she wasn't sure what, exactly.

They did enjoy the pedal boats, but Allison wasn't certain if such a late time in the afternoon would be the best time for the lake. She'd decide when she got there. One thing she did know was that, since the twins had their binoculars, perhaps some limited bird-watching and maybe more nature identification using the books Shane had given them would help them pass the time. It would also be a step in the right direction for her to guide the girls' first visit back to the grounds, maybe even giving them a few pointers about how to read trailheads and the colored trail markers on the map at the headquarters entrance.

She definitely wasn't going to lose anyone this time.

"Kids, I'll be right back," Mia called to the older ones as she helped Allison and the twins to the car. In no time, they had each girl in her booster seat. "Looks good." Allison stepped back after double-checking that Isla's buckle was snapped into place. She reached into her driver's side to start the car and tune the radio into a station the girls liked.

"Bye, Miss Mia!" Isla blew her a kiss, which Mia pretended to catch. She threw one back through the air to Olivia, who responded with the same.

"Bye, girls!" She waved again, then closed the door of the Honda with the air conditioner running before looking at Allison over the top of the car. "Can I talk to you for a minute?"

"Sure." Allison glanced again at the girls to make sure they were secure before walking around to the passenger side.

Mia stayed where she was, angling her back to the car in order to talk more clearly to Allison. Lowering her voice, she said, "I read the emails that came through this week from CASA. About the girls' mother making plans to terminate her rights."

Allison nodded.

"Do you know why?"

Allison had her suspicions. Perhaps the twins' mother was spurred by their recent birthday or their completion of kindergarten. Those milestones were major ones, so it would be reasonable for someone to reflect on that. But their mother had also been fighting demons of her own, ones that weren't abating, from what Allison understood through things shared in the court system and by Nancy. "She hasn't stopped using."

Drugs were hard demons indeed.

It was Mia's turn to nod. "So when this all goes through..."

"I have no idea how long that will be."

Mia didn't seem concerned with the timeline. "You know that I love them. Michael and I both do, and we always will."

Allison felt exactly the same.

"But—"

Allison placed her hand on Mia's forearm to stop her from having to say what she knew she would. "But this arrangement is temporary, I know. That's all it was ever going to be."

Mia reached for Allison's hand, siphoning shared strength. "Promise me they won't get lost in the system."

Allison made a vow. "I won't let that happen." She didn't know what the coming months would look like and what would eventually play out in court. But Allison was all-in with these girls. Through the good, bad and all the uncertainty, she would stand by them.

And love them fiercely.

She knew their foster parents did, too. And their foster siblings. And others in the Cottonwood Creek community as well, like their kindergarten teacher, CASA volunteers and fellow kids in the system they had met at The Saturday Stroll. Their network was increasing, and in the absence of a mother's physical presence, they had love coming at them from all sides.

Allison's heart hurt for their mother, not only because of her struggles with drug use but also because of her emotional journey. Surrendering parental rights could not have been an easy decision, and from an outsider's perspective, it could look a lot like abandonment. But even in the fog of addiction, it seemed that the twins' mother wanted what was best for the girls. Providing that—through terminating her rights—was actually a very definitive act of love.

If she ever needed to find a way to underscore that for the girls, she would. In spades. Someday, the time would come for that.

That heavy conversation, though, was for another day. Today was all about having fun and giving the girls meaningful childhood experiences.

"You're such a good person." Mia leaned in for a hug, adding, "And you'll make a great mother yourself someday."

Allison stiffened. As kind as the words were, they hit hard. The truth was she still wasn't sure if she ever wanted to be a mother. How was a woman even to know?

Mia pulled back, sensing Allison's reticence. "Did I say something I shouldn't have?"

"No," Allison insisted, forcing a smile. "It was nice of you to say." She stepped back and placed her hand on the car's door. "Now I need to get these girls to the park."

"Of course. Good luck."

"Thank you. We'll be back no later than seven."

"Enjoy your time with them."

"I always do," she said, which was true. Because even though Allison wasn't their mother and in spite of the setback on Saturday, she still had nothing but fondness and affection for the pigtailed six-year-olds who were happily lip-synching to some radio tune from the backseat of her car. Oh, those girls! Their happiness was effervescent and seeing that in these unexpected ways as they grew was a gift that Allison was honored to witness.

She walked back around, opened her driver's door, settled herself in and notified the girls with an "Away we go!" send-off. One final time, she checked her mirrors to make sure Lucky hadn't escaped from the house before she pulled out of the driveway. With an all-clear thumbs-up from Mia back by the front door, Allison and the twins headed on the familiar route to Cottonwood Creek State Park.

On the way, the song the girls had been singing ended, and the airwaves switched to a commercial. Allison lowered the volume.

"I'm starting to like the park." Isla pumped her legs that dangled from the extra height given to her from her booster seat as she looked out the window.

"Me, too," Olivia chimed in. "Will we see Mr. Shane there?"

Allison looked at the girls through her rearview mirror. "Why do you ask that?"

"Because I like him."

"Me, too."

"I guess we'll see," Allison responded, her eyes back on the road. Then, privately, she couldn't help but agree with the twins. *I like Shane, too.*

Shane closed the laptop, cleared his desk and stood up for a much needed stretch. Opening the door of his office after the west Texas job interview and stepping into the park's headquarters, he was greeted by Nadine, who couldn't hide her disdain at Shane being locked in his office for so long. "That was a lengthy meeting."

Shane had remained vague with Nadine earlier in the day and hadn't divulged that it was a job interview. She knew he had applied for the job but not that today's interview was happening. Why worry Nadine about something like that anyway, especially since he wasn't sure how it was going to turn out? He thought about telling her now that it was over, but decided in the moment to keep mum. It wasn't the right time; not until everything was official.

Just in case.

Instead, he gave a generic reply. "You know how the park system runs things."

"Bureaucrats." Nadine scrunched her face. She had no love lost for bureaucracy, though, in truth, her actions of being employed by the parks system betrayed her current critique.

"Just remember those bureaucrats are keeping us employed."

"They don't know how lucky they have it with people like us."

"I hope they do." Shane mentally replayed some moments of the interview. He had done his best and felt like he could walk away from it satisfied with his performance. The ultimate decision was now up to the board.

In the meantime he needed to get back to business, checking on all the things in the park that needed his attention now that he was no longer tied to the computer. "I'm going to make the rounds."

"Garrett left at four o'clock. So check all the sheds," Nadine advised.

"Will do. I'll make sure they're locked for the night."

Nadine nodded as Shane pushed open the door to the first real sunshine he had seen in hours.

It never failed. The outdoors always felt good.

With the sun on his face and breezes at his back, he started meandering toward the three storage sheds scattered throughout the park, waving to visitors and answering a few questions from various patrons as he did.

"Shane!"

"Shane!"

Hearing the high-pitched double dose of his name could only mean one thing.

"My favorite twins." He raised his sunglasses as the girls came running to him.

"Look what we found." Olivia held up a rock with a circular indentation. "Allison said it's a fossil."

"Am I right?" She was just a few steps behind the girls.

"Let's have a look." Shane accepted the rock, rubbed his thumb over the concave spot, making an exaggerated effort of considering the find before announcing, "She's right. It's a fossil."

"Wow!" The girls seemed more excited than if they had found gold.

"It's from a snail."

"How do you know that?" Olivia asked.

"Let me show you." He bent down and pointed out the

shell portion, explaining how time, pressure and nature had resulted in this treasure.

"I've never seen a fossil before." Isla was as wide-eyed as her sister.

"They're not in our book," Olivia pointed out.

"Well then..." He pressed the rock back into Isla's hand before standing up. "We'll just have to get you a book that does show them, won't we?"

"Yes!" Both twins nodded.

"That's very generous." Allison put her hands on the girls' shoulders as she looked to Shane with a sentimental smile. "You've already done a lot."

This might be the last act of generosity he bestowed on the girls, and the realization of that tightened his stomach in a way he hadn't expected.

"Are you okay?" Allison noticed his distraction.

Shane dropped his hand and snapped back to the moment. "Sure thing." He blinked twice, stowing his sunglasses on the front pocket of his uniform before looking directly at Allison, that pit in his stomach growing. "Can I talk to you for a minute?"

"Sure." Her voice was reticent as she asked, "With the girls? Or—"

"Just you. Give me a couple of minutes?" Until he saw her, he hadn't realized that she was the first person he wanted to tell about the interview. Emotions overtook him, and now he wanted to share everything.

Including the hardest part: the truth.

He owed it to her to tell her he had an interview for the west Texas job. That much was clear.

Less clear was how she would respond to the news of him actually leaving.

Chapter Sixteen

Allison, Shane and the girls were in the shade of a magnificent, hundred-year-old oak tree.

"Girls," Allison said, placing her hands on the twins' shoulders, "can you go sit against the trunk while Shane and I talk for a minute?" The distance was just enough to keep them out of earshot but within her line of sight.

"Adult stuff?" Olivia asked, wise beyond her years.

"Because we know that sometimes adults have to talk to each other. Without kids around." Isla thumbed the fossil in her hand.

"Yes, please." She turned the girls in the right direction. Allison wasn't entirely sure what Shane had in mind when he asked to talk, but having the girls' attention focused elsewhere would be safe. "We won't be long." She asked the twins to sit crisscross and also to check their animal book for other things they wanted to look for on their excursion.

"Okay." The girls bounded happily toward their new spot, skipping along before settling down as Allison turned back to Shane.

"What did you want to talk to me about?"

He lifted his hand to his shoulder, rubbing a spot on his neck.

But he didn't say anything.

Or, if he did, Allison didn't hear it.

She was distracted. He was silhouetted by the late-afternoon sun. She tried not to stare, but she couldn't help herself. He was every bit as handsome as he'd been since they met, but with a vulnerability today that made her focus on him in a way she hadn't felt herself doing before.

There was definitely an ache in his eyes, a look that caught Allison equally off guard. "Shane?"

"Allison?" He lowered his arm, squaring his stance in front of her. Steady eye contact willed her to look at him.

She did.

And everything else seemed to fall away.

"I need to tell you something." Shane's eyes did the rest of the talking, a concentrated look that put Allison in a trance. If he didn't say something else soon, her knees were going to go weak, and she might just melt before this man in uniform, who was doing something to Allison's equilibrium.

When Shane's arm moved a fraction of an inch toward her, she instinctively moved her own, their hands colliding in a surprise position.

Into one another's.

He seemed as shocked as she did, both breaking their gaze to look down at their sudden handhold and then back up to one another again. "Allison?" he started once more, her name like a summons on his lips.

She couldn't hold back any longer.

Answering that call, she leaned toward Shane, closing the distance between them. Her lips landed softly on his, a sweet moment that was everything she wanted—and didn't know she did.

Shane didn't pull back, but he didn't deepen the kiss. Instead, their spontaneous contact came to a sudden end thanks to a high-pitched duet coming from nearby.

"K-I-S-S-I-N-G!" The twins' singsong was enough to make both Shane and Allison jump back from each other and immediately stop what they were doing.

Allison's mind reeled from the kiss she was so happy happened.

A kiss.

With Shane.

It was Allison's turn to try to make sense of the moment. She had acted on intuition, on impulse that had been weeks in the making. How had she not seen it until this moment? Shane was a gentleman, a man who wasn't necessarily going to say things that his heart was feeling. But he had a way of making his intentions known.

Allison had read him well.

She wasn't sorry about the kiss.

"That shouldn't have happened." When Shane said those words out loud, Allison's disappointment washed over her, leaving her to wonder what was really going on.

He shouldn't have let her kiss him.

"I'm sorry." Regret flashed in his mind as he choked down feelings that he was having a hard time placing.

The six-year-old twins moved closer, giggling, forcing Shane's attention away from Allison and onto their wide smirks of interest. Suddenly, this sight was much more entertaining to them than finding fossils or watching for birds.

"Girls!" Allison admonished, more embarrassment in her tone than scolding.

"I fear I gave you the wrong impression." He needed to own up to his mistake.

Allison was preoccupied with shushing the girls, waving her arms in a cut-it-out motion that just made them giggle harder.

"That wasn't talking," Olivia observed. "You said you were going to be talking."

Shane walked to where they were standing, bent down on one knee and crouched to their level. They shuffled closer to him, big smiles on their faces. He kept his own face serious, however, because he wasn't going to undermine her. He wanted to be honest.

With all three of them.

Shane started speaking to the girls, but he looked up to Allison as he did so. "There's a lot to like when it comes to Allison. She's smart and kind. Hardworking and generous."

"She's really nice," Olivia cut in.

"And very pretty," Isla added.

"Yes." Shane met Allison's memorable topaz eyes as she looked at him over the tops of the girls' heads, her cheeks reddening. "That she is." Wisps of hair that had fallen from her ponytail lifted and lowered on the breeze, framing her face. She didn't need makeup or fancy lighting to look good. Against a natural backdrop and with all of the confidence she exuded simply by being in her own beautiful skin, she was stunning through and through.

There was no shortage of attraction on Shane's side of the equation when it came to Allison.

But the absence of a tangible future between them was something he couldn't ignore. "But I might be leaving Cottonwood Creek soon."

"Where are you going?" Olivia asked, innocence flowering over her face.

"Far away to another state park. If I get the new job I applied for."

"Can we come there?" Oblivious to the wide geography of Texas, Isla asked the question.

"Maybe one day for a visit. But it's too far for me to keep working here at Cottonwood Creek."

"Why?" Olivia tilted her head.

"Yes," Allison echoed, her voice soft and her question gentle. "Why?" A hint of moisture appeared in the corners of her eyes as she spoke, her brief words heavy with emotion.

He rose instinctively at the sight of her on the verge of tears but kept his distance when he saw her posture stiffen. Instead, he gave her space and answered with the honesty she deserved. "This job was always supposed to be temporary. My dream is to work in west Texas."

"That's your dream?" Allison swiped at her eye with the edge of her hand. "I didn't know." Allison shook her head, too apologetically for Shane's taste.

"No," he urged. "It isn't something you would have known. I should have told you right away." His heart filled with regret. This wasn't the best way to tell her, and certainly the timing was not ideal after a kiss.

Shane's stomach bottomed out on that realization as well, the high of his professional success destroyed by this personal failure. He was letting three people down—three people whom he cared about so very much.

Allison had dealt with emotional highs and lows more times in her life than she cared to count.

So had the twins.

And even though they weren't comprehending everything that was happening in regard to this conversation between herself and Shane, the girls understood enough.

They liked Shane.

They had trusted Shane.

And they were losing him.

That betrayal was unforgivable to Allison. Fiercely protective of these girls whose hearts were fragile and whose futures were uncertain, she had done everything she thought she could do to support and protect them.

Having them see her kiss Shane and then having him abandon them felt like being pushed off a cliff. "Girls, we should get going." Allison willed her own tears to stop, telling herself to replace the disappointment she had felt just moments ago with an entirely opposite emotion.

Indifference.

Shane had sought out time with her—while all this time he'd been planning to leave? He wanted her to commit to future Saturday Strolls—that he wasn't even going to be around to see? He'd kissed her—knowing he was walking away from Cottonwood Creek forever?

Some people could never be trusted. Not her father. Not her ex. And certainly not Shane.

"Please," Shane said. "Don't go."

The word *go* echoed in her ear like a bad country song. "Look, we don't have a lot of time this evening. The girls have things they want to see in the park." Allison's focus on them helped her put aside her own emotions, which was exactly what she needed in order to stay standing. Her legs weren't going to hold her upright for much longer if she just stood still. "But congratulations on your job interview."

"Thank you." His words sounded as empty as their future.

Weeks ago, Allison didn't even know Shane. Now she considered him her partner in The Saturday Stroll and, she thought, a friend she could trust. Even so, she didn't have any notions of romance with this ranger.

Then their kiss had changed things.

Because a kiss meant a great deal to her. In that moment, a future had been possible.

Then, just like that, it wasn't.

Their relationship was over before it even had a chance to really get off the ground, and that hurt Allison as much as anything that Shane had said.

There was nothing left to do but focus on the girls. After all, that was why she came to the park late this afternoon in the first place.

But the girls had other ideas.

"Mr. Shane?" Olivia tugged at the corner of his uniform shirt. "Do you want a cookie?" Olivia looked up at him, her face shining with innocence. She offered him the plastic bag of homemade chocolate chip cookies she had been carrying, now no doubt a bit gooey since they had all been traipsing around in the park.

"You know..." He smiled in spite of the heaviness of everything that just happened. "I would absolutely love a cookie. Thank you, Olivia."

"I made them, too." Isla mirrored her sister, who sat down crisscross on the grass to open the bag. "Try the one that looks extra bumpy. It's got a lot of chips."

"Good tip, Isla." He reached his hand inside the bag. Their moment was serene, with him and the twins involved in this spontaneous peace offering.

Watching them, Allison's emotions threatened again. Her eyes burned as salty tears welled up. She looked away to blink them back, and when she returned to face the scene again, they were each happily munching on a cookie, the twins flanking Shane one on each side as he also sat crisscross. A park ranger in full uniform was somehow as flexible as two six-year-olds.

Tough on the outside, he could be soft when it came down to it.

"Allison," Olivia called to her, waving the bag. "Try one." Isla also urged her to join them.

And in spite of everything that Allison felt and everything in that moment that was telling her to feel nothing, she couldn't help but walk toward the twins, accept a cookie herself and sit down across from Shane to create a foursome, a sad reminder to her of a gathering that wouldn't be happening again.

Chapter Seventeen

The air inside the medical clinic smelled even more antiseptic than usual.

Or Allison's nose was reacting to things differently.

Ever since Friday, her senses felt off-kilter. The weekend hadn't done much in the way of rejuvenating her. But energized or not, Monday's responsibilities rolled around without consideration for her emotional state.

She hadn't talked to Shane all weekend or gone back to the park. She was on hiatus from both of those things until he left for good. If she was being honest with herself, her heart had a crack in it that she didn't know how to repair.

She would resume her runs at Cottonwood Creek State Park after Shane left, when there was no threat of running into him. Besides, her muscles could use a break, and she'd swap outdoor exercise for indoor exercise. She could put on a stretching video at home. Perfect timing with the hot Texas summer in full swing anyway.

So she told herself.

The Saturday Strolls? Those would be dealt with…later. A new head ranger would be hired by September, so there was no use in working on anything until then. But work at the clinic was another story. She found her rhythm there as she always did, settling into the routine of tasks that she knew and problems that she could solve. It felt better to focus on her brain instead of her heart.

At the end of the day, she noticed three missed calls from Nancy on her cell. "Hey, Nancy, what's going on?" she asked as she called her from inside her car before she left the medical clinic parking lot.

"Are you sitting down?"

"Yes." Allison had nowhere else to move inside the driver's seat of her Honda.

"Good."

Allison's skin prickled. "You're scaring me."

"I couldn't leave this in a message. You needed to hear it straight from me."

"Okay..." Allison had spoken to Nancy plenty of times, but she had never heard her tone quite like this.

"It happened, Allison. The twins' mother signed over her rights. Officially. The girls are eligible for adoption as of today."

Allison clamped her hand over her mouth. It was one thing to know the process was in motion. It was an entirely different thing to hear that it had happened.

"The judge signed off in district court late this afternoon. When these things happen," Nancy explained, "you know they can happen fast."

"I'll say." Allison's free hand dropped to her lap, and she had to be careful not to let her other do the same. "Do Mia and Michael know?"

"Not yet. My next call is going to be to them. They need to know this but, Allison," Nancy's voice carried an urgency, "I wanted to ask you an important question before I do."

"Yes?" Her breath caught as her adrenaline increased.

"Those twins need a mother, and their placement in foster care was always temporary. We all knew that."

Allison nodded on the other end of the line.

"Before this case gets legs of its own, I want to know from you..." Nancy paused, speaking with clarity through the line that was hard to mistake. "Do you want to apply to be their adoptive mother?"

If Allison had anywhere to collapse, she would have done so because no moment in her life had felt this meaningful, this transformative.

Motherhood? Her?

She was speechless.

Nancy had rendered her so with this news. But it really wasn't about her.

It was about Olivia and Isla.

Flashes of their sweet faces replayed in her mind, her memories and her experiences with them. She had known the girls for a fraction of their lives, but for such a big part of their most important memories. She had been there when they started school for the first time. When they went on their first boat ride. When they blew out their candles at their only birthday celebration. She knew their quirks, Olivia's reticence at times and Isla's grittiness. They could be stubborn, and they could be boisterous. They could be whimsical and sometimes shy but still so expressive.

Their futures before coming to Cottonwood Creek were uncertain, but here, they flourished and thrived. Allison saw it in their mannerisms and in their movements. Mia and Michael expressed as much, too. So did their kindergarten teacher.

"That's a big question." Allison put one hand on her chest, rising and falling as she took in the news.

"Yes," Nancy said, "and I don't ask it lightly."

"I know that."

They remained silent on the line together while Allison's

mind ran circles around this conversation. She had so many questions. "Is a condition of their adoption that they would stay in Cottonwood Creek?"

"No." The blunt answer hit with hurricane force. "There is no next-of-kin who has stepped up, so whoever adopts them can settle them elsewhere."

"But their home..." Allison thought about their school, their friends, the Westmoreland kids, their dog Lucky, everything they now knew. "It's here. In Cottonwood Creek."

"It is now," Nancy agreed. "But they need a parent. And that parent is free to choose where they go."

"Even if that means..." The girls not being near Allison was something she'd always known was a possibility. "Even if that means that they leave Cottonwood Creek?"

"Yes."

That answer knocked the wind out of Allison in a way she hadn't expected. She gripped the phone harder, trying to understand all these moving parts. The theory was one thing; that she understood from her CASA training and her experience. But the reality of it when it involved the twins—two girls whom Allison loved as if they were her very own— was something else.

The silence on the line made Nancy ask, "Allison, are you still there?"

"Yes, I'm here." Her voice sounded so far away, even to her.

"Think about it," she urged. "You don't have to answer now but—"

"Yes." The word sprang from Allison's lips, an answer that had been months in the making. Love made a family. Allison may not have much figured out, and maybe the court system wouldn't even accept her application. She had never wanted to be a mother, but now was different.

Her life was different.

Pushing her fears and her prior plans aside, she had already made room in her life for the girls. How the future would look for them all was uncertain, but wasn't the future always so? Allison had a job, she had time for them and she had endless love to give them both. The girls had willingly given that to her, too. Allison was sure of it. She had felt it for months, whether she chose to recognize it as such or not.

Love. That was what made a family.

"Yes," she repeated, this time stronger and louder, convincing herself fully as she did. The double affirmation, shocking as it was to Allison's own ears, felt absolutely right in her heart.

And that was how she knew it was the answer.

"Yes, I want to adopt the girls." Allison straightened her spine, sitting up as tall as she could and confirming, "Yes, I want to be their mother."

"You were supposed to be here for four months," Nadine said as she crossed her arms and frowned at Shane.

"That was the plan." Shane shifted his weight to his back leg. "But plans sometimes change."

The two were in a standoff in his office after he told Nadine the news that he had been asked to officially take the job in west Texas.

"When do you start?" Nadine tapped her foot, still frowning.

"July fifteenth." The wheels of the park system administration could move so slowly at times and so swiftly at others.

"It's going to be hot. Out there where you'll be."

"All of Texas is hot."

"Not like west Texas."

"The nights are cooler."

"Says who?" Nadine cut her eyes at Shane.

He wasn't going to debate her. "Look, there are some things I'll like, and there are probably some things I'm not going to like."

"More snakes. Less grass. Landscapes that are brown and brown and brown." She uncrossed her arms as she enumerated more dislikes before Shane stopped her.

"Whoa, whoa, whoa." He put up his hand. "I get it."

She stopped counting, her tone changing. "You don't have to leave."

"Is that emotion I hear in your voice, Nadine?" Shane teased her, knowing when she was feisty and when she wasn't.

She nodded, maybe unwilling or maybe unable to mince words.

It seemed Nadine had a soft spot after all.

"Mr. Atacosta," she reminded Shane, "was here twenty years before retirement. Think about that."

Shane held the thought in his mind, just as Nadine continued.

"Twenty years," she repeated again. "And why do you think that was?"

"I haven't a clue."

"You do," she challenged him.

"Is that so?" Hearing the certainty in Nadine's voice that he was wrong was a new experience for him.

"Because this place is special. The landscape, the people, all of it."

"There are special people and places everywhere."

"Not like this town." Nadine left no room for argument.

"Okay," Shane conceded, "I'll admit that I do like it here. I even like my coworkers." Shane winked, but Nadine didn't react. "But all I was ever supposed to be here was an interim park ranger. You know that as well as I do."

"Then don't be an interim. Be a permanent park ranger. Problem solved."

"It's not that simple."

"Men make everything so complicated—" Nadine blew out a breath "—when it doesn't have to be. It really can be simple."

"If you're so certain of that, then what's the answer?" Shane put the question to her more in jest than in seriousness.

Yet, she didn't answer it with a joke. She answered it simply.

"Stay. That's all you have to do," she said, the words as plain as if the answer was something he could have said himself.

But none of this was plain or simple.

Shane was being pulled in two different directions. Which one was right for him?

He wished he knew.

Decisions in Allison's life had always been made meticulously.

She thought about things.

She planned for the process.

She took steps toward the outcome.

Leaving home? Check. Moving to her own place? Check. Starting college? Check. Finishing college? Check. Getting a job? Check.

Being a mother?

That had never been on her to-do list, at least not permanently.

When she would see a mother happily pushing her baby in a stroller or encounter a young family in the aisle of the grocery store, she would sometimes wonder to herself, "What if?"

But that was all they were. Thoughts.

In her mind, the reality of becoming a mother had always involved a relationship first. Falling in love, then marriage, then starting a family.

But as a CASA volunteer, she'd seen that sometimes things went differently for different people. Not everyone took the same path.

For instance, Mia was a mother, both biological and foster. Allison had seen her be a model of care and love, doting on the twins and giving them everything she could, regardless of whether she gave birth to them or not. Nancy, too, was a loving and supportive mother to her only daughter, who was now in college herself. Dr. Zambrano had two children. She managed to not only be good at her job but also to thrive at the clinic she worked hard to build. So many of Allison's co-workers were also mothers, who managed both their home and work lives successfully.

So it could be done.

Not everyone—like her father—walked away from parenthood when the going got hard.

Allison had more in common with her own mother and with the women around her in Cottonwood Creek than she did with the father who'd left her behind.

On the one hand, she didn't know the first thing about motherhood but, on the other, she knew everything she needed to know. Most importantly, it was possible. Love made everything so.

When she told Nancy yes over the phone, she put into motion a path that was a bit terrifying but that also, somehow, felt so very right. Saying yes had been easy because, as Allison's heart told her, this was the right move.

Now, would the court agree? Would this actually happen?

She gave herself up to the process, knowing that she could control certain things, but not the outcome. That part took a healthy dose of faith. She could chew her fingernails down to the quick on the uncertainty, or she could do what she had always done.

Plan for the process.

And take steps toward the outcome.

She had a whole community of strong women as role models to help her.

And she planned on leaning on them—and God—for support.

She didn't need to go it alone.

Chapter Eighteen

The hot asphalt seemed to steam into the air of the late afternoon, mile after mile passing beneath the wheels of Shane's Ford pickup. He hit the gas and rode with the windows down, wind whipping into the cab as he headed for home.

His temporary home.

That was what Cottonwood Creek was for him. He had carved out a comfortable little space in a corner of it, long enough to live, work and plan the next part of his life.

So why was Nadine's advice to change that plan causing him so much inner turmoil? He could hear the last word she said to him over and over in his mind.

Stay.

She made it sound so simple.

But being in one place never was.

He learned that from growing up. Staying in one place meant being stagnant, giving in to a life that was not in line with what he valued. Leaving, by contrast, meant he could build the life he wanted, in the place he wanted.

The more distance he could put between his past and his present, the better.

Up until this job at Cottonwood Creek, everything had moved forward. He worked hard, and he was finally being rewarded for that in a way that guaranteed his professional success. Like his west Texas friend Troy, Shane was now going to be a permanent, full-time ranger, in charge of acres of unspoiled land as far as the eye could see. He was to be the steward of natural beauty on God's green earth that he could secure for generations into the future.

Shane Hutton had been called, and he was needed in the west as much as he needed that place.

So why, then, did it feel like there was a war raging inside him? Was he supposed to fight? Or flee?

Because, as he thought about his decision, it felt strangely like he was doing the latter by running to west Texas. His parents didn't need to understand that. Nadine didn't need to understand that.

Or Allison.

But he wished, of all people, that she did. Maybe if he had told her sooner, she would have found a way.

That was what hurt the most. Coworkers would carry on. The parks system would find someone this week for the permanent position at Cottonwood Creek.

But he kept thinking about Allison. He had hurt her, that much was clear. The light that dimmed in her eyes after their kiss when he told her about the job was hard to forget.

Then there were the twins.

Olivia and Isla had been strangers to him just a few short weeks ago. He had no nieces or nephews of his own, no little brothers or sisters in his biological family. So when these little princesses kept crossing his path, his heart had opened to them. It was like life wasn't even giving him a choice in the matter.

He cared for them.

That was a foreign feeling.

So much of his time in Cottonwood Creek was like that. He'd expected one thing, and experienced something else.

Even the geography was different in reality than he had fully understood from vague perceptions, like this stretch of land that took him home.

He pulled over to the side of the roadway, parking his truck on the shoulder and taking out his cell phone. Scrolling through his contacts, he punched a familiar number.

"Hi, Shane." Hearing Troy's voice was what he needed. "What's going on, buddy?"

"So much. Got a minute?"

"Always."

Shane's eyes panned the tall stalks of johnsongrass that waved from the roadside. "I've been thinking a lot about west Texas."

"I know you have. I'm excited about you finally being out here." Shane's absence of a reply made Troy fill the void. "You are coming out here, aren't you?"

"I need to figure some things out."

"Talk." Troy's offer was immediate. "I'm all ears."

As Shane talked, he didn't have to give details about the job offer he received and the general timeline since Troy had been privy to that. He had been with Shane every professional step of the way.

"What's holding you back?" Troy asked.

Troy listened as Shane filled him in on Allison, the twins and admitted his feelings for the first time aloud. "There's something about this place."

"There's something about that *place*," Troy repeated, "or is there something about *her*?"

Shane knew the answer to that.

As he talked more with his friend, he continued to take in the landscape by the roadside where he had pulled over. It was dotted with silvery dandelions and goldenrod cattails.

Surprise pops of color were there for discerning eyes that took time to see them, the yellow lantana and bright orange flowers atop butterfly plants, the deep purple wine cups and blush-pink primroses peeking up from ditches. He hadn't noticed how pretty this stretch of roadway was until...

"Troy?"

"Ya, buddy?"

"You know my plan has always been a kind of one-way ticket."

"I know."

Shane thought about the state he loved. Texas was nearly eight hundred miles east to west. Driving across it took a traveler about thirteen hours. Plenty of Texans never make it to all parts of the state in their lifetime. Shane had plans to reach the edge.

But plans change.

"Are you happy where you are?" Shane asked his friend.

"I'm happy. The bigger question is—" Troy swallowed a breath "—are you?"

Shane gripped the steering wheel tightly to try to feel his way through a decision he couldn't outrun.

"I am happy," Shane admitted.

"Where?"

Shane rolled his shoulders back, sitting up taller as he answered with conviction that had been building inside him. "Here." The admission created a calm in him that settled over every inch of his body. "Here in Cottonwood Creek."

"Then I think you better tell someone about that."

Shane agreed with his friend, and knew what he had to do.

West Texas wasn't where he needed to go anymore. No, there was a more important place he needed to be.

He just hoped she would be there when he drove up.

***

Allison was looking forward to doing nothing else on Monday night but crawling into bed early in her pj's with a pint of chocolate ice cream.

After the call with Nancy, she took some preliminary steps through email when she got home, but she would have to lean on the legal process for the rest. Nancy was calling Mia and Michael with the news, and Allison would follow up to coordinate with them for the best way to talk to the twins.

As much uncertainty as there was about the process, there was also calmness that enveloped Allison these past few hours, wrapping her in a blanket of security that felt like a hug from an angel.

It was about time she felt like that.

Yet, decisions were Allison's to make in moving forward with the adoption process for the girls. She thought about that as she moved through her house with her ice cream pint in hand, taking small bites to help her contemplate it all.

She had agreed to being the girls' mother, or at least trying to be. Now she needed to work with Nancy to take the next steps legally.

Allison knew the ins and outs of the adoptive process through being involved with CASA. What she didn't know was how often the local courts granted adoption to a single woman. None of the girls' relatives had stepped forward, but would that change at the last minute? And what of her own desires about motherhood? Those had shifted, but Allison still wanted to do right by the twins. Could she do that in their formative years to come?

Time would provide answers, but tonight all she wanted was some peace and quiet, and a night to process it all. She balanced the pint of chocolate ice cream and a spoon in one hand, before crawling into sheets that felt as fresh as a summer breeze.

The balm of her comfortable bed always worked to soothe her, both body and mind.

But even best-laid plans got interrupted.

Suddenly, she heard the deep, unmistakable triple ring sounding from her front door.

An evening package delivery? Maybe. Some neighborhood kids playing a prank? Possibly. Either way, investigating now was better than wondering later, so taking her ice cream with her and her spoon just in case she needed an impromptu weapon, she strode to the front door, kicking her running shoes out of the way as she opened to an unexpected visitor who had never before come unannounced.

"Shane." She opened the door but kept herself protectively hidden behind it. "What are you doing here?"

"Hi, Allison." His handsome profile and broad chest were no less attractive in the dim light of her entrance.

"I didn't expect you."

"I'm sorry. But I needed to see you."

"Okay." Allison leaned toward the jamb, waiting for clearer words.

"I need to make a choice."

Those words were no clearer than his surprise visit.

"That's not true." He shook his head and shifted toward the jamb as well. "I've already made the choice. Allison…" He looked at her, his countenance a map of emotion. "I told you I was going to west Texas, but that's not accurate."

"Oh?"

"No, it was." His words jerked against her own fuzzy thoughts. "But plans change."

"What's going on, Shane?"

He took a deep breath. "I don't want to go to west Texas. I

mean," he tried again, "I wanted to, but that was in the past. My present is…" His eyes roamed as he fought to find the words when his eyes darted to what she was holding halfway behind the door. "Is that ice cream?"

Allison whipped her head toward her hand, the pint peeking over the edge of the wooden door, the handle of the shiny silver spoon pointing right at Shane. "Chocolate fudge," she confirmed.

"Good choice." Shane's chest rose and fell, his voice taking a break as Allison waited for his next move.

The ranger uniform that Allison had seen on him more often than not stood in contrast to her lounge pants and T-shirt that she was still sheepishly trying to hide. But she couldn't hide her manners, especially when it involved a friend. "Would you like some?" She tilted the pint toward him.

"Can I come inside if I say yes?"

"Is that what you want?"

"Very much." Shane blew out a long breath. "So very much."

Allison stood up straight, her messy ponytail bobbing. Opening the door fully, she showcased it all—bare feet, casual clothes, no shred of makeup—her natural, relaxed self. The vulnerability of standing before him in such a way hit at her very core.

"I need to, um…"

Shane's focus continued. His own face wore a look Allison had never seen on him, an expression not just of interest but of something deeper.

He didn't blink, yet his eyebrows lifted and lowered as they both stopped in their tracks before each other. "This feels…" he said softly, his voice trailing as Allison shut the door behind them.

"Cold." She looked to her ice cream, the temperature of it

freezing her palm and fingers. Shane noticed, and he scooped his hand around hers, taking the pint to give her relief and settling it on the edge of the entry table.

"Better?"

She shook her still-cold hand through the air that was heating up between them. "Thank you."

Shane took her hand in his, warming it. Allison melted with his considerate touch, allowing herself to be absorbed in the unexpected moment.

Hand in hand, they stood, locked together in touch and thought.

He pulled her toward him, slipping one hand onto her waist as a flutter of adrenaline ran through her body. "You always have the best ideas. In fact—" he took her chin in his hand and raised it to fully meet his gaze "—you're the one who helped me see that the best ideas are the ones right in front of my eyes."

Steadily, she extended one of her hands toward his shoulder while the other pressed to his chest. "I…" The words wouldn't come, but the feelings did.

Shane's voice rose like a lifeline, and she grabbed hold, her hands settling more confidently onto his body when he said, "I want to talk to you about turning down the west Texas job."

"Why is that?"

"Because I want to stay here, in this town. With people that I care about." He held her in his arms, willing her to listen to his every word.

"What people?" There was nowhere else she wanted to be because standing chest to chest with Shane Hutton—even in her most vulnerable state—felt natural and good.

"You." His eyes pierced the air that charged between them as he said again, "I want to be wherever you are, Allison."

That admission was matched by his actions, this sudden closeness. And yet, Allison couldn't help but ask, "We haven't started anything. Have we?"

"This started when I wasn't even looking for it. And now that it has," he paused a moment before continuing, "I don't want to end this. I don't want to leave. I want to..." His voice trailed, his lips searching for the word that he then said like a punctuation mark. "Stay."

"You're staying in Cottonwood Creek?" Even with this late-night admission, Allison needed to be sure she understood. "Permanently?"

"As permanently as the park system will have me."

"But you're an interim park ranger, aren't you?"

"I have to give it a shot to apply here. And I can. If—" His lip twitched before he said, "As long as you'll tell me that you want me to stay, too."

Stay.

One word.

It's all she had to say.

Allison did want that. But even her heart couldn't override her head. "I do want you to stay, but it's not just me anymore." She looked down, her voice quiet. "I may be a package deal."

Shane's palm moved across her arm, a gentle caress. "What do you mean?"

"The twins." She raised her head, meeting Shane's warm gaze. "I'm applying to become their adoptive mother."

A sparkle in Shane's eyes spread, followed by a wide grin that stretched across his face. "That's amazing, Allison." His whole countenance lit with enthusiasm, no hesitation in his words. "Because no one would make a better mother than you."

Of all the compliments anyone had ever given her, that one hit the deepest.

"And if you'll let me, I'd like to be with you on that journey. However you'll have me, whatever support you'll let me give and whatever this—" he glanced down at them both "—ends up being. I'm not leaving, Allison. This is my home."

Epilogue

"Look at me, Allison! I did it myself!" Olivia looped both thumbs through her life jacket, beaming at Allison. Lucky looked approvingly from his end of the leash that Olivia held.

"Great job." Allison double-checked the buckles to make sure they were all secure. "How is yours coming, Isla?"

"Almost…got it…" She stuck her tongue between her teeth, chewing on it as she looked down with laser focus to the last plastic buckle. Allison bent to her level, but only to be there if she needed her. Isla figured it out on her own, with an unmistakable satisfying click. "I did it!"

Every little success was cause for celebration.

"We like being on the boats." Olivia and Isla had both been asking about a return to the lake, and another adventure in the pedal boats seemed like a good idea, especially now that the girls were so much more familiar with the park.

And Allison.

These past few months had brought about a much closer relationship between them as they awaited their formal adoption by Allison. Perhaps one day the girls would call her Mom, but until that time, even just hearing her name from their lips was an act of love that filled Allison with warmth every time they spoke.

The girls had started first grade, and their independence

was increasing every day. Much to Allison's delight, their sense of outdoor adventure was also taking hold, even with the change of seasons. "Let's go, Allison." They started toward the boats but waited on her. With her life jacket also firmly in place, she extended both her hands as the girls rushed to her to grab hold, one on each side. She stood at the center of them, like three units of a chain. They were bound, with a bond just as strong.

Not bound by blood.

Nor biology.

But by love alone.

As long as they shared that, there was nothing in the world that could break that bond.

"Which one should we pick? Yellow, red, or blue?" Allison swung the girls' arms as they strode toward the available boats.

"Yellow!"

"I want blue!"

Maybe giving them a choice in everything wasn't the best route.

She'd learn the best route when it came to future situations like that. For now, she made a plan. "How about we close our eyes, spin ourselves around and the first boat I see when I open mine is the one we'll take. Deal?"

"Deal!" The twins squinted their eyes shut and threw their hands in the air, pirouetting round and round like ballerinas. Allison had no choice but to follow suit; this was her idea, after all. Laughing to herself, she closed her eyes and turned in a couple of carefree circles, letting her arms helicopter from her torso.

Having fun with these two would never get old.

Grinding to a quick stop, she popped open her eyes, which landed on...

"Shane!" The girls' voices called in unison to the uniformed ranger coming their way, a life jacket swinging from his hand. Suddenly, the choice of pedal boat was secondary to this happy visitor walking to join them.

"Hi, girls," he called, raising his free hand over his head in a hearty greeting.

They rushed over to him, flitting like butterflies as he smiled broadly at them and then at Allison.

"What are you doing here?" She raised her hand to block the sun from her eyes.

"Coming to see my girls," he answered, as if it was the most natural thing in the world. As he bent down to greet the twins, they threw their arms around his neck, covering him in a double dose of affection. They couldn't talk to him fast enough.

"We were going to pick a boat—" Isla started.

"And Allison had an idea," Olivia cut in, "that we close our eyes and then—"

"Because that's what we do for hide-and-seek."

"I'm talking about the boats."

"I know." The girls' words tripped over one another, covering Shane in an explosion of conversation that had him grinning from ear to ear.

"I wanted the yellow—"

"Blue for me!" Isla raised her hand.

Shane chuckled at their unstoppable energy.

Olivia twisted toward Allison and asked, "Which one did you pick?"

"Yeah," Isla urged, "what did you see first?"

What did she see?

That was a good question.

Allison took in the scene before her: a handsome, trusted man who embraced two little girls who were brimming with love. She saw comfort and safety. She saw hope and adventure. She saw everything she never knew she had been wishing for. A sweet calm spread in the air among them all, a dance of absolute childhood delight and wonderment.

"This, this is what I saw." She strode toward the trio, opening her arms as they waddled in their life jackets back to her, hugging her legs and looking to her for a better answer.

But as far as Allison was concerned, she had all the answers she needed. Her heart was full, and her future was brimming with possibility. The twins' futures were, too.

Cottonwood Creek had become their home. The twins had people who cared about them, including Allison's mother, who was always at the ready with activities, support and one-on-one time.

The other relationship that had grown stronger over the past few months was the one between Shane and his parents. He had reached out to them with a phone call after making the decision to stay in Cottonwood Creek, which led to some heartfelt conversations and more communication between them. Over the past few months, they had already made one trip from their home outside Huntsville to see him. Shane seemed at ease around them, and they were as charmed by the community as much as Shane was.

Cottonwood Creek was a good home.

Shane had made this place his, just as Allison had done. Now they could enjoy it together. As she looked to him, he flashed an appreciative gaze, his face brimming with a warmth that filled her up.

The girls let go of her legs. "Mind if I tag along on the boat?" he asked.

"Please! Please!" The girls' pleading added to Shane's question.

Allison surveyed three eager faces, all bursting with joy. "How can I say no to that?"

"Yay!" The twins jumped, cheered and even raised a couple of fist pumps into the air.

She knew how they felt.

Happy news made her heart leap, too, and happy occasions were always cause for celebration. Even the simplest of situations could do that.

Like time outside.

Having an adventure together.

And doing it with loved ones.

"Shall we?" Shane gestured toward the red boat. "A chariot on the water awaits my girls."

Allison extended her hands again, but this time, Shane grabbed hold of one, Olivia grabbing his and Isla grabbing Allison's. The four of them walked toward the pedal boat, the sun shimmering on the water as they strode hand in hand, an unbreakable chain.

* * * * *

Dear Reader,

Welcome to Cottonwood Creek, Texas! Thank you so much for reading.

I've always been a traveler. I love the experience of a new place, especially beautiful, sweeping outdoor spaces. That's why I enjoy state parks. And when I can't go there in real life, I relish being an armchair traveler.

I hope you, too, enjoyed traveling by book as you read Shane and Allison's story. While Cottonwood Creek State Park is fictional, aspects of it are based on real state parks throughout Texas. The state has nearly ninety of them, from east to west and north to south. Texas is a big state!

The community and the landscape that surrounds Shane and Allison help them build their connection. Comfortable places have the power to do that. Places can make us feel at home as much as the people in them.

Wherever you live and whomever you surround yourself with, I hope you feel like my characters: safe, accepted and loved. I appreciate you visiting Cottonwood Creek, and I hope you'll come back.

Audrey Wick

Get up to 4 Free Books!

We'll send you 2 free books from each series you try PLUS a free Mystery Gift.

FREE Value Over $25

Both the **Love Inspired**® and **Love Inspired**® **Suspense** series feature compelling novels filled with inspirational romance, faith, forgiveness and hope.

YES! Please send me 2 FREE novels from the Love Inspired or Love Inspired Suspense series and my FREE gift (gift is worth about $10 retail). After receiving them, if I don't wish to receive any more books, I can return the shipping statement marked "cancel." If I don't cancel, I will receive 6 brand-new Love Inspired Larger-Print books or Love Inspired Suspense Larger-Print books every month and be billed just $7.19 each in the U.S. or $7.99 each in Canada. That is a savings of 20% off the cover price. It's quite a bargain! Shipping and handling is just 50¢ per book in the U.S. and $1.25 per book in Canada.* I understand that accepting the 2 free books and gift places me under no obligation to buy anything. I can always return a shipment and cancel at any time by calling the number below. The free books and gift are mine to keep no matter what I decide.

Choose one: ☐ **Love Inspired Larger-Print** (122/322 BPA G36Y)   ☐ **Love Inspired Suspense Larger-Print** (107/307 BPA G36Y)   ☐ **Or Try Both!** (122/322 & 107/307 BPA G36Z)

Name (please print)

Address   Apt. #

City   State/Province   Zip/Postal Code

Email: Please check this box ☐ if you would like to receive newsletters and promotional emails from Harlequin Enterprises ULC and its affiliates. You can unsubscribe anytime.

Mail to the **Harlequin Reader Service:**
IN U.S.A.: P.O. Box 1341, Buffalo, NY 14240-8531
IN CANADA: P.O. Box 603, Fort Erie, Ontario L2A 5X3

Want to explore our other series or interested in ebooks? Visit www.ReaderService.com or call 1-800-873-8635.

---

*Terms and prices subject to change without notice. Prices do not include sales taxes, which will be charged (if applicable) based on your state or country of residence. Canadian residents will be charged applicable taxes. Offer not valid in Quebec. This offer is limited to one order per household. Books received may not be as shown. Not valid for current subscribers to the Love Inspired or Love Inspired Suspense series. All orders subject to approval. Credit or debit balances in a customer's account(s) may be offset by any other outstanding balance owed by or to the customer. Please allow 4 to 6 weeks for delivery. Offer available while quantities last.

Your Privacy—Your information is being collected by Harlequin Enterprises ULC, operating as Harlequin Reader Service. For a complete summary of the information we collect, how we use this information and to whom it is disclosed, please visit our privacy notice located at https://corporate.harlequin.com/privacy-notice. California Residents – Under California law, you have specific rights to control and access your data. For more information on these rights and how to exercise them, visit https://corporate.harlequin.com/california-privacy. For additional information for residents of other U.S. states that provide their residents with certain rights with respect to personal data, visit https://corporate.harlequin.com/other-state-residents-privacy-rights/.

LIRLIS25